Book of

FUN,

Facts, and
Science

Farrar Straus Giroux Books for Young Readers
An imprint of Macmillan Publishing Group, LLC
175 Fifth Avenue, New York, NY 10010

Printed in China by RR Donnelley Asia Printing Solutions Ltd.,
Dongguan City, Guangdong Province
Designed by Gegham Vardanyan

First edition, 2018
1   3   5   7   9   10   8   6   4   2

mackids.com

ISBN: 978-0-374-30943-5

Disney A WRINKLE IN TIME

Book of

FUN,

Facts, and Science

Written by AUBRE ANDRUS

DR. ANNMARIE THOMAS, CONSULTANT

Illustrations by ALBERTO MADRIGAL
AND NIKOLAY TUNIMANOV

FARRAR STRAUS GIROUX • NEW YORK

Why hello there, Earth Warriors!

YOU LOOK LIKE YOU'RE UP FOR AN
ADVENTURE. AND WE NEED HELP!

MEG, CALVIN, AND CHARLES WALLACE
COULD USE ANOTHER GENIUS AS THEY
FIGHT THE DARKNESS AND BRING LIGHT
TO THE UNIVERSE.

COME ALONG AS WE TRAVEL THROUGH
SPACE AND TIME CRACKING CODES,
SOLVING PUZZLES, UNVEILING THE TRUTH,
AND GENERALLY, WELL, SAVING THE WORLD.

DON'T FEAR THE UNKNOWN. BE BRAVE!
BE A WARRIOR!

GOOD LUCK,

Mrs. Whatsit
Mrs. Who
Mrs. Which

"WE ARE OUR LIGHT AND OUR DARK

$E=mc^2$

$E = hv = \dfrac{hc}{\lambda}$

$p = mv$

MADE WHOLE BY OUR LOVE."

—Mrs. Who

Character Crossword

Use the clues below to fill in the blanks in this crossword puzzle.

Across

1. He wanted to find the origin of the universe and shake its hand.

2. She can change sizes.

3. He loves expanding his vocabulary.

4. She speaks in quotes.

5. His greatest gift is his empathy.

Down

6. Her favorite planet is Uriel.

7. He sees visions.

8. She wears a locket with her dad's photo inside.

9. The Murry family dog.

1 Across: Dr Murry

2 Across: Mrs Which

3 Across: Charles wallace

4 Across: Mrs who

5 Across: calvin

6 Down: Mrs Whatsit

7 Down: Happy Medium

8 Down: Meg

9 Down: for libras

Answers on page 138

9

Story Starter

"It was a dark and stormy night" is a famous opening line of two books from the 1800s that author Madeleine L'Engle reused for the beginning of *A Wrinkle in Time*. Start your own novel below using the same first sentence.

It was a dark and stormy night. _____

_____

_____

_____

_____

_____

_____

_____

_____

_____

_____

_____

_____

_____

_____

_____

_____

_____

Which Planet Is Which?

These clues will help you decipher the names
of the planets that appear in Meg's universe.

1 This is the first planet to which Meg tessers.

RULIE Uriel

2 Meg gets a warm hug from a furry creature that
lives on this planet.

CHILEX Ixchel

3 Meg travels here to save her father, Dr. Alex Murry.

ZATCOZAM Camazotz

4 Meg meets the Happy Medium on this planet.

ROONI Orion

5 Meg, Charles Wallace, and Calvin call this planet home.

HARTE Earth

Scared of Storms?

Thunderstorms frighten Meg, which is why she leaves her lonely attic bedroom and heads downstairs to the kitchen. Luckily, Charles Wallace is ready to comfort her with some warm milk and sandwiches. If Meg had known exactly when the storm was coming, she might have felt a little better.

You can tell how far away a storm is by counting the time between the lightning and the thunder. Lightning causes thunder. You can't have one without the other!

Light travels faster than sound. This is helpful when using the "flash-to-bang method" for determining when a storm is coming. Count the seconds between a lightning flash and the thunder that follows. Then divide that number by 5. That's about how many miles away the storm is.

1. If you counted 30 seconds between a flash of lightning and the rumble of thunder, how far away is the storm?

2. If you counted 15 seconds between a flash of lightning and a rumble of thunder, how far away is the storm?

3. If you counted 5 seconds between a flash of lightning and a rumble of thunder, how far away is the storm?

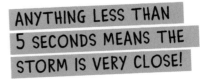

ANYTHING LESS THAN 5 SECONDS MEANS THE STORM IS VERY CLOSE!

Answers: 1. Six miles; 2. Three miles; 3. One mile

COLOR MRS. WHICH

Mrs. Which is wise and loving. She's actually a few billion years old! Use your imagination and color in her dress.

Read Someone's Mind

Charles Wallace knows the feelings and thoughts of those around him. You can make it seem like you've read someone's mind using these simple math tricks. After telling your friend to pick a number and perform these equations, no matter what number your friend picked, the answer your friend gets will always be a five or a three, depending on which set of equations you use. Try it with a friend.

Arrive at Five

1. "Pick a number, but don't say it aloud."
2. "Multiply that number by 2."
3. "Add 10."
4. "Divide by 2."
5. "Now subtract the original number."
6. "Your answer is 5!"

I See a Three

1. "Pick a number, but don't say it aloud."
2. "Double that number."
3. "Add 9."
4. "Subtract 3."
5. "Divide the answer by 2."
6. "Now subtract the original number."
7. "Your answer is 3!"

Science Buzzword Word Search

Mr. and Mrs. Murry spend their lives researching how to tesser across multiple dimensions. See if you can spot all the important buzzwords from their research below.

```
A S Q O P Z L A O D F E E M C O E J G P
R T O D E O N X E I P C H L U S V I E A
A X O I S K H D E E L H A S Z C O T Y R
Y E V M A T H Q O U F T Y B T I M E C E
E A M E W P B O R R T A C S O E M S E H
H I W N N X A S A Z Y M I K I N F S O L
W Q E S B E N X O P A E R R U C B E I M
T R R I N W R A A H N F I K D E S R D E
E A I O L I U G A R C Z L P E D W A S Z
U I S N X Y A A Y M I S L O O Q U C H Y
O Y F F K L O L B O M I P I U O T T J E
W E V U I L O A H P E E S A L M E A F O
I N J O A A E X C E Z U N B C Y L A W P
Q R A I M E W Y E G G T L M X E A A O K
D D R O I K W N B L U N I V E R S E P I
O L L A S Q O I Z M P B M Y U H K H B T
H E O D D V I R B N A E O I T M E K S S
F A R V I B R A T I O N S S N O T S J A
M R G G E X I Z E N L K O C H R A A T W
A N O L I G H T E R A W E J A Q U I T S
```

ATOM	LIGHT	QUANTUM	TIME
DIMENSION	LOVE	SCIENCE	UNIVERSE
ENERGY	MATH	SPACE	VIBRATIONS
GALAXY	PHYSICS	TESSERACT	WRINKLE

Answers on page 138

Connect the Dots

Everything is not as it seems on Uriel. Flowers can talk, people can fly—what else will Meg find? Follow this dot-to-dot to reveal Meg's favorite part of this special planet.

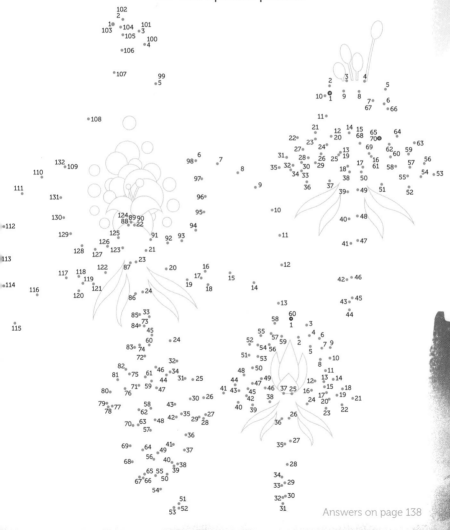

Answers on page 138

Dr. ALEX MURRY

Occupation: THEORETICAL PHYSICIST AND NASA SCIENTIST

Location: UNKNOWN

Publications: CO-AUTHOR OF *THE TESSERACT: STRINGS, MULTI-DIMENSIONS, AND FREQUENCY* WITH BIOPHYSICIST DR. KATE MURRY

Research Interests: "I WANT TO TOUCH THE STARS AND UNLOCK THE SECRETS OF THE UNIVERSE."

Multi-Dimensions

Dr. Alex Murry is obsessed with researching the dimensions of space and time, which helps him discover how to tesser. Tessering allows people to travel great distances by folding space and time.

THE THREE DIMENSIONS

Every physical object has three dimensions: length, width, and height (or depth). To find out how much space, or volume, an object takes up, you can multiply length by width by height.

LENGTH (X), the longer of the two horizontal dimensions

WIDTH (Y), the shorter of the two horizontal dimensions

HEIGHT (Z), the vertical dimension

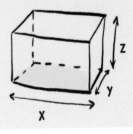

$E=mc^2$

$E = h\nu = \dfrac{hc}{\lambda}$

$p = mv$

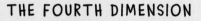

THE FOURTH DIMENSION

Time is the fourth dimension, and one of the reasons Meg can't find her dad, Dr. Alex Murry. Even if she knows *where* he is, she doesn't know *when* he is!

THE FIFTH DIMENSION

According to Dr. Alex Murry, a straight line is not the shortest distance between two points—not if you use the fifth dimension, which is outside the rules we know of time and space. Unfortunately, Dr. Alex Murry disappeared before he could write it down!

FAST

FASTER

Uriel
Mrs. Whatsit's
favorite planet.

PLANET

Orion
Where the Happy
Medium hides
in a cave.

Camazotz
Home of the IT and
purely evil energy.

MAP

Ixchel
Mrs. Who's home.

Earth
Home of Meg,
Charles Wallace,
and Calvin.

The ENFoLDer

"Not gone, just enfolded." That's what Meg says when she plays with this enfolder—there's a heart hidden inside. Meg's dad gives it to her before he disappears, so she keeps it close during her journey to find him. Make your own by following these steps.

YOU WILL NEED:

- PAPER
- MARKERS OR COLORED PENCILS
- SCISSORS
- GLUE STICK

TRACE: Take a piece of paper and trace the pattern on pages 24 and 25. Then, cut it out.

COLOR: Color in the enfolder. The light blue sections will fold together to create the heart shape. Make sure to color those sections the same color.

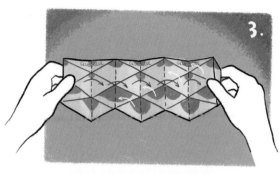

FOLD: First, crease the dashed lines by folding them forward. Then crease the diagonal lines by folding them backward.

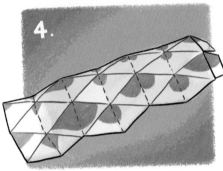

MATCH: Match the dots by gently folding the paper. The heart pattern remains on the outside.

GLUE: Add glue to the designated edges and press them firmly together. Let dry.

PRESS: Add glue to the end tabs. Press each end of the paper firmly together. Let dry.

The Enfolder

GLUE GLUE GLUE

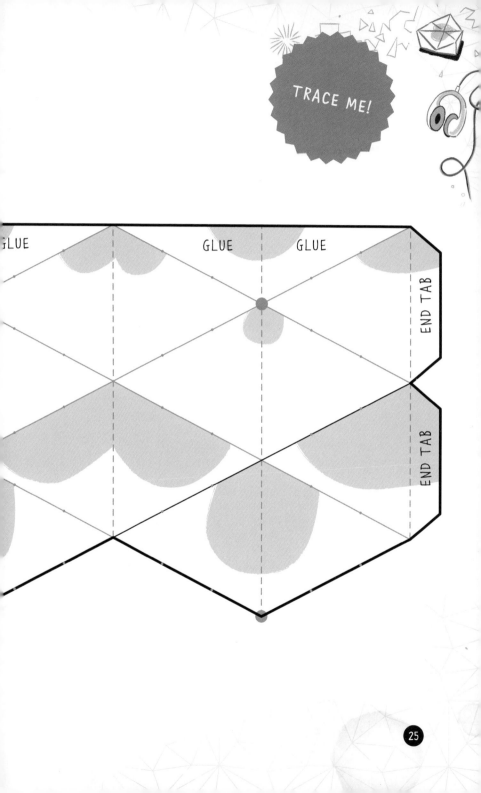

TRACE ME!

GLUE　　　　GLUE　　　GLUE

END TAB

END TAB

The Fifth Dimension

Many scientists—including Meg's own parents—believe that time travel could be possible. The question is, how do we do it? Decide whether the following statements about time travel are true or false. Don't know something? Look it up!

TRUE   FALSE

1. Albert Einstein believed shortcuts existed through a space-time continuum that we now call "wormholes."

2. According to physicists like Stephen Hawking, the key to traveling to the future is figuring out how to travel as fast as the speed of light.

3. Traveling to the future involves the same science as traveling to the past.

4. E = mc² proves that time travel is possible.

5. Time-travel machines exist today, but they can only move people a few minutes into the future.

6. The fastest any human has traveled is about 25,000 mph on the Apollo 10 moon mission in 1969.

7. A clock in space ticks slightly slower than a clock on Earth.

8. Black holes and wormholes are the same thing.

9. Meg's parents believed the universe is made of vibrating quantum fields that connect everything.

Answers: 1. T; 2. T; 3. F; 4. T; 5. F; 6. T; 7. T; 8. F; 9. T

Time Travel

The Mrs.'s and the kids travel almost instantly through space and time by tessering, which means finding a "wrinkle" in time. If you could tesser to anyplace in the world during any time in history, where would you go and why?

_____

_____

_____

_____

_____

_____

_____

_____

_____

_____

_____

_____

_____

_____

_____

_____

_____

_____

_____

_____

Meg's Room

Meg needs to organize her room.
Can you help her find each of these
missing objects?

GLASSES

LOCKET

ENFOLDER

BACKPACK

EINSTEIN BOBBLE HEAD

CALCULATOR

EXPANDING SPHERE TOY

Answers on page 138

Sketch a Locket

Meg wears this locket every day, and inside she keeps a photo of her father. Design a new locket for Meg to wear in which she can keep a picture of her whole family.

Find Your Place in the Universe

Are You More of a Meg or a Charles Wallace?

Meg and Charles Wallace were raised in the same house, but they sure have a lot of differences. Answer these questions to see which character you are more like.

1. WHICH SOUNDS MOST LIKE YOU?

A I feel like I can read people's minds.

B I'm great at solving puzzles.

2. I BELIEVE THAT . . .

A anything is possible.

B everything should be questioned.

3. PEOPLE OFTEN THINK THAT I . . .

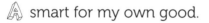 know everyone because I'm friendly.

B am shy just because I'm quiet.

4. WHEN I SEE SOMEONE GET BULLIED, I . . .

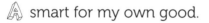 stand up for them and say something.

B get really mad.

5. WHICH DESCRIBES YOU MORE?

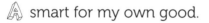 I can talk to anyone.

B I'd rather keep to myself.

6. PEOPLE SAY THAT I AM TOO . . .

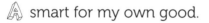 smart for my own good.

B hot-tempered for my own good.

7. I SHOW MY LOVE THROUGH . . .

 words.

B actions.

Answers on page 139

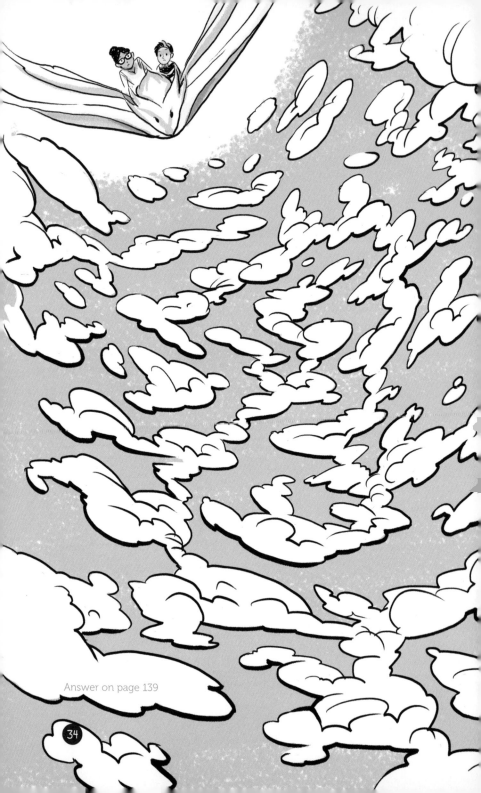

Answer on page 139

Flying Through Uriel

Calvin gets separated from Meg and Charles Wallace as they fly through the air in Uriel. Find the fastest path so Meg can save her friend from falling.

Which Mrs. Said Which?

Mrs. Which, Mrs. Whatsit, and Mrs. Who are an interesting bunch. See if you can match up the Mrs. to the correct quote. There are three quotes for each Mrs. character.

MRS. WHATSIT

The friendly Mrs. W who leads the kids on an adventure.

MRS. WHICH

Sometimes small and sometimes tall, but always wise and loving.

MRS. WHO

Curiously, speaks in quotes, and wears diamond glasses.

1.
"Wild nights are my glory!"
Mrs. W_____

2.
"That which is seen is temporal. That which is unseen is eternal."
Mrs. W_____

3.
"Is there such a thing as a wrong size?"
Mrs. W_____

4.

"We're warriors, serving the light and good of the universe."
Mrs. W_____

5.

"The only thing faster than light is the darkness."
Mrs. W_____

6.

"Everyone knows flowers are the universe's best gossipers."
Mrs. W_____

7.

"You must not be afraid to be afraid."
Mrs. W_____

8.

"Don't you realize the trillions of events that had to occur since the birth of our universe to lead to the making of you exactly as you are?"
Mrs. W_____

9.

"Once you've seen what is unseen, it is yours."
Mrs. W_____

PERIODIC TABLE

H 1 Hydrogen 1.0								
Li 3 Lithium 6.9	Be 4 Beryllium 9.0							
Na 11 Sodium 23.0	Mg 12 Magnesium 9.0							
K 19 Potassium 39.1	Ca 20 Calcium 40.1	Sc 21 Scandium 45.0	Ti 22 Titanium 47.9	V 23 Vandadium 50.9	Cr 24 Chromium 52.0	Mn 25 Manganese 54.9	Fe 26 Iron 55.9	C Cob 58.
Rb 37 Rubidium 85.5	Sr 38 Strontium 87.6	Y 39 Yttrium 88.9	Zr 40 Zirconium 91.2	Nb 41 Niobium 92.9	Mo 42 Molybdenum 95.9	Tc 43 Technetium 99	Ru 44 Ruthenium 101.0	Rl Rhod 102
Cs 55 Cesium 132.9	Ba 56 Barium 137.3	Lanthanides 57-71	Hf 72 Hafnium 178.5	Ta 73 Tantalum 180.9	W 74 Tungsten 183.9	Re 75 Rhenium 186.2	Os 76 Osmium 190.2	Ir Iridiu 192
Fr 87 Francium 223	Ra 88 Radium 226	Actinides 89-103	Rf 104 Rutherfordium 267	Db 105 Dubnium 268	Sg 106 Seaborgium 271	Bh 107 Bohrium 272	Hs 108 Hassium 270	M Meitne 27

La 57 Lanthanum 1.0	Ce 58 Cerium 1.0	Pr 59 Praseodymium 1.0	Nd 60 Neodymium 1.0	Pm 61 Promethium 1.0	Sm 62 Samarium 1.0	E Europ 15.
Ac 89 Actinium 227	Th 90 Thorium 232	Pa 91 Protactinium 231	U 92 Uranium 238	Np 93 Neptunium 237	Pu 94 Plutonium 242	Ar Americ 24

$E = h\nu = \dfrac{hc}{\lambda}$

$p = mv$

oF ELements

								He 2 Helium 4.0

B 5 Baron 9.0	C 6 Carbon 12.0	N 7 Nitrogen 14.0	O 8 Oxygen 16.0	F 9 Fluorine 19.0	Ne 10 Neon 20.2
Al 13 Aluminum 17.0	Si 14 Silicon 28.1	P 15 Phosphorus 31.0	S 16 Sulfur 32.1	Cl 17 Baron 32.1	Ar 18 Argon 40.0

i 28 le 7	Cu 29 Copper 63.5	Zn 30 Zinc 65.4	Ga 31 Gallium 69.7	Ge 32 Germanium 72.6	As 33 Arsenic 74.9	Se 34 Selenium 79.0	Br 35 Bromine 79.9	Kr 36 Krypton 83.8
d 46 ium .4	Ag 47 Silver 107.9	Cd 48 Cadmium 112.4	In 49 Indium 114.8	Sn 50 Tin 118.7	Sb 51 Antimony 121.8	Te 52 Tellurium 127.6	I 53 Iodine 126.9	Xe 54 Xenon 131.3
t 78 um .1	Au 79 Gold 197	Hg 80 Mercury 200.6	Ti 81 Thallium 204.4	Pb 82 Lead 207.2	Bi 83 Bismuth 209	Po 84 Polonium 210	At 85 Astatine 211	Rn 86 Radon 222
s 110 dtium 1	Rg 111 Roentgenium 280	Cn 112 Copernicium 235	Nh 113 Nihonium 286	Fl 114 Flerovium 289	Mc 115 Moscovium 288	Lv 116 Livermorium 293	Ts 117 Tennessine 294	Og 118 Oganesson 294

d 64 ium 3	Tb 65 Terbium 158.9	Dy 66 Dysprosium 162.5	Ho 67 Holmium 164	Er 68 Erbium 167.3	Tm 69 Thulium 168.9	Yb 70 Ytterbium 173	Lu 71 Lutetium 175
n 96 ium 7	Bk 97 Berkelium 247	Cf 98 Californium 251	Es 99 Einsteinium 254	Fm 100 Fermium 253	Cf 101 Mendelevium 256	No 102 Nobelium 254	H 103 Lawrencium 257

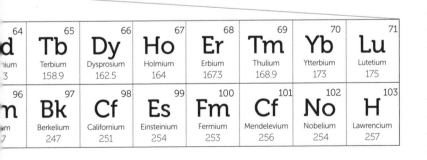

Design Your Own Planet

Meg sees a lot of strange things on her travels—from interesting flowers on Uriel and unusual beasts on Ixchel, to the darkness of Camazotz and the caves of Orion. If you could name and design a planet, what would it be? Draw it below.

What is the name of your planet?

_____

Does your planet have a sun or moon? How many?

_____

What do the trees and plants look like?

_____
_____
_____

Can animals or humans be found on this planet?

_____

What is the weather like? Are there seasons?

_____
_____
_____

Are there mountains, oceans, or deserts on your planet?

_____
_____
_____

What kind of laws have to be followed?

_____
_____
_____

Fibonacci Sequence

WHAT IS IT?

It's a series of ascending numbers, with the next number found by adding up the two previous numbers. 0, 1, 1, 2, 3, 5, 8, 13 . . .

$$0 + 1 = 1$$
$$1 + 1 = 2$$
$$1 + 2 = 3$$
$$2 + 3 = 5$$
$$3 + 5 = 8$$
$$5 + 8 = 13$$

WHO WAS FIBONACCI?

Leonardo Pisano, otherwise known as Fibonacci, was a famous mathematician. In the 1200s, he published a book that made popular the 10 numbers we use today: 1, 2, 3, 4, 5, 6, 7, 8, 9, and 0.

Fill In the Blanks

Can you complete the series of numbers below?

0	1	1	2	3	5	8	13		34
55		144	233		610	987		2,584	4,181
6,765		17,711		46,386		121,393	196,418		514,229

Answers: 21; 89; 377; 610; 1,597; 10,946; 28,657; 75,025; 317,811

18,201

8,248

6,765

5,020

13,907

4,181

10,946

5,793

3,234

2,584

20,377

17,711

15,130

7,113

3,943

Connect the Dots

20,563

1,780

25,244

2,330

1,597

1,650

64

101

30

28,657

33   21   13

9

987

34

8

43,375

93

1   1
0
2   5

18

55   112   3

443

830   610

89

Complete this dot-to-dot puzzle by connecting **only** the Fibonacci sequence numbers from lowest to highest.

121

310

46,368

144   233   377   731

56,254

212

The Fibonacci sequence can be turned into a logarithmic spiral, which can be used to describe certain shapes in nature like the nautilus shell, the arrangement of seeds in a sunflower, and a spiral galaxy.

75,025

99,333

80,637

118,037

121,393

143,135

194,420

160,996

282,351

196,418

Answer on page 139

226,582

Overcome IT

Meg learns firsthand that the IT can transform the hope and joy within us into things like pain, fear, and jealousy. What makes you happy? Keep a running list here so you can confidently fight the feelings brought on by the IT.

Color Mrs. Who

The first time Meg sees
Mrs. Who, she's surprised
by her diamond glasses.
They sparkle so brightly,
Charles Wallace might
call them *luminous*.
Color in Mrs. Who
and her colorful
quilt.

Meg's Notebook:
3-D Shapes

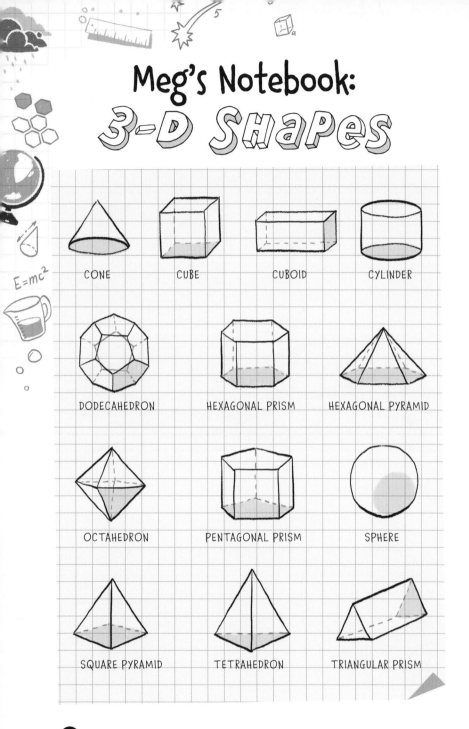

CONE

CUBE

CUBOID

CYLINDER

DODECAHEDRON

HEXAGONAL PRISM

HEXAGONAL PYRAMID

OCTAHEDRON

PENTAGONAL PRISM

SPHERE

SQUARE PYRAMID

TETRAHEDRON

TRIANGULAR PRISM

$E=mc^2$

Doodle 3-D Shapes

How do you make a two-dimensional drawing look 3-D? Here are a few step-by-step instructions that will make your doodles pop off the page.

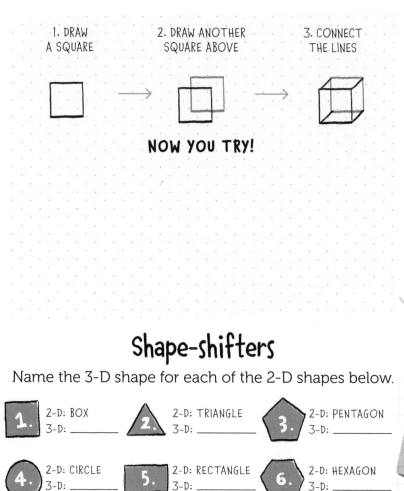

1. DRAW A SQUARE   2. DRAW ANOTHER SQUARE ABOVE   3. CONNECT THE LINES

NOW YOU TRY!

Shape-shifters

Name the 3-D shape for each of the 2-D shapes below.

1. 2-D: BOX
3-D: _____

2. 2-D: TRIANGLE
3-D: _____

3. 2-D: PENTAGON
3-D: _____

4. 2-D: CIRCLE
3-D: _____

5. 2-D: RECTANGLE
3-D: _____

6. 2-D: HEXAGON
3-D: _____

1. Cube; 2. Square pyramid; 3. Pentagonal prism; 4. Sphere; 5. Cuboid; 6. Hexagonal prism

Find the Differences: GALAXY

The universe is filled with galaxies of all kinds—there may be as many as 100 billion! Look closely at the galaxy on the left and compare it to the galaxy on the right There are 10 differences to spot. Circle them all.

Answers on page 139

Up, Up, and Away!

Meg, Charles Wallace, and Calvin are able to fly on Uriel with the help of Mrs. Whatsit who transforms herself into a flying creature. Meg tries to explain the phenomenon of "lift" to Calvin—it's the upward force that keeps things in the air, from a kite to an airplane. See how much you know about flying by choosing the correct answer below.

1. SIR ISAAC NEWTON'S FIRST LAW OF MOTION STATES THAT FOR EVERY ACTION THERE IS . . .

 an equal and opposite reaction.

B no reaction.

2. AIR IS INVISIBLE . . .

 and it weighs nothing.

B but it does have weight.

3. HELIUM BALLOONS FLOAT BECAUSE HELIUM IS . . .

 lighter than air.

B heavier than air.

LIFT

THRUST

DRAG

GRAVITY

4. THRUST IS THE FORCE THAT _____ AN OBJECT IN MOTION.

A propels

B slows

5. DRAG IS THE FORCE THAT _____ THE OBJECT IN MOTION.

A aides

B opposes

6. IF A PLANE'S THRUST IS GREATER THAN ITS DRAG, IT WILL:

A Continue moving

B Stop

Dr. KATE MURRY

Occupation: BIOPHYSICIST

Location: AN URBAN CITY ON EARTH

Awards: NATIONAL SCIENCE FOUNDATION AWARD

Publications: CO-AUTHOR OF THE *TESSERACT: STRINGS, MULTI-DIMENSIONS, AND FREQUENCY* WITH NASA SCIENTIST DR. ALEX MURRY

Research Interests: "THE SMALL. THE ATOMS, PARTICLES, AND UNSEEABLE ENERGIES THAT MOVE THROUGH US ALL."

WHAT'S AN ATOM?

Dr. Kate Murry loves studying very small things like atoms. They're so small you can't even see them with your naked eye! Everything you know—including yourself—is made up of atoms.

Atoms are the building blocks that form an element, like oxygen or hydrogen. Atoms can also link up to form molecules, which can group together to form compounds or cells, which can combine to create larger things like humans or planets or galaxies. A compound is something that is made of two or more separate elements.

Imagine an ice-cream store that sells 118 different flavors of ice cream. Each flavor is an element, just like you'd see on the Periodic

Table of the Elements. And each scoop is an atom. If you put two or more scoops of chocolate ice cream together, you've formed a molecule. If you put two or more scoops of different flavors together, like chocolate and vanilla, you've formed a compound.

Molecule Match-Up

Study the illustrations of elements and compounds below and see if you can match them up to the correct name. Hint: The letter on each scoop of ice cream helps reveal the answer!

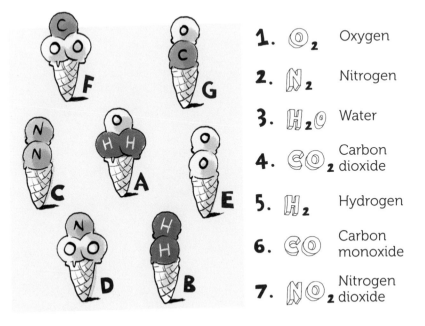

1. O_2 Oxygen

2. N_2 Nitrogen

3. H_2O Water

4. CO_2 Carbon dioxide

5. H_2 Hydrogen

6. CO Carbon monoxide

7. NO_2 Nitrogen dioxide

Scientific Method

The scientific method is an organized process that helps solve a problem or answer a question. Meg's parents use it to create a theory on tessering involving vibrations, light, and love.

$E=mc^2$

ASK A QUESTION: WHAT'S THE PROBLEM?

↓

MAKE OBSERVATIONS: WHAT DO YOU ALREADY KNOW?

↓

CREATE A HYPOTHESIS: WHAT IS A POSSIBLE SOLUTION?

↓

EXPERIMENT TO TEST YOUR HYPOTHESIS: WHAT'S THE CAUSE AND THE EFFECT?

↓

MAKE A CONCLUSION BASED ON THE DATA

SCIENTIFIC THEORY
A proven explanation based on the results of many experiments.

DO YOU ACCEPT THE HYPOTHESIS? WRITE A THEORY!

DO YOU REJECT THE HYPOTHESIS? FORM A NEW HYPOTHESIS!

Now, you try!

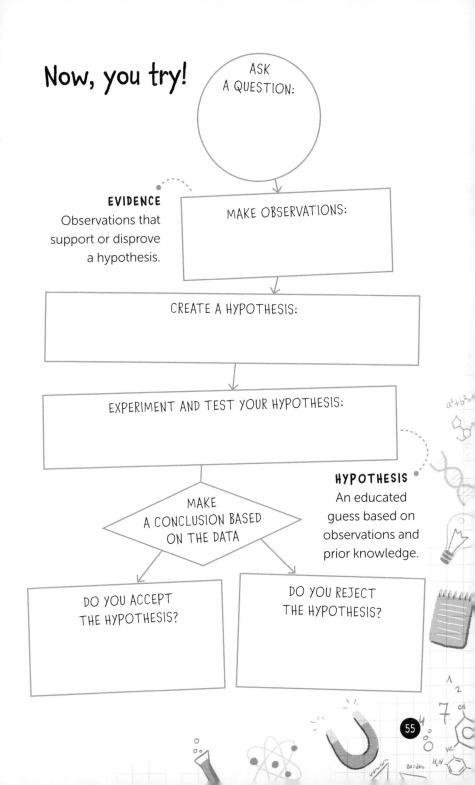

ASK A QUESTION:

MAKE OBSERVATIONS:

EVIDENCE
Observations that support or disprove a hypothesis.

CREATE A HYPOTHESIS:

EXPERIMENT AND TEST YOUR HYPOTHESIS:

MAKE A CONCLUSION BASED ON THE DATA

HYPOTHESIS
An educated guess based on observations and prior knowledge.

DO YOU ACCEPT THE HYPOTHESIS?

DO YOU REJECT THE HYPOTHESIS?

Balance Is the Key

The Happy Medium helps people find balance within themselves. He can also tap into cosmic energy to help find answers to questions. See if you can find your own balance.

Write answers to these questions.

What is unbalanced in your life?

_____

_____

_____

How can you fix it?

_____

_____

_____

What questions do you want answers to?

_____

_____

The Mrs.'s Do Math

1 Day = 24 Hours	1 Minute = 60 Seconds
1 Hour = 60 Minutes	1 Foot = 12 Inches

1. Mrs. Who only speaks in quotes, and she speaks about eight quotes per hour. If she wakes up at 9 AM and goes to bed at 9 PM, how many quotes does she say per day?

2. Mrs. Whatsit wants to give the Happy Medium a message. She only has 1 hour to spare and it takes 10 minutes total to tesser to and from Uriel. How long can she visit with the Happy Medium?

3. Mrs. Which is sometimes very tall and sometimes very small. If she starts at 105 feet tall, but wants to shrink to Meg's size at 5 feet, how many inches must she shrink?

Answers on page 139

Map the Universe

Use the coordinates on the **X** and **Y** axes to answer the questions below.

1. Put a heart on M7. This is where Meg's dad is!

2. Meg's final tesser is to F2. What's there?
_____

3. Which planet can be found at H3?
_____

4. Draw a flower on L3. What's there?
_____

5. Where can Ixchel be found?
_____

6. Draw a shooting star on C7.

7. Where is Mrs. Whatsit?
_____

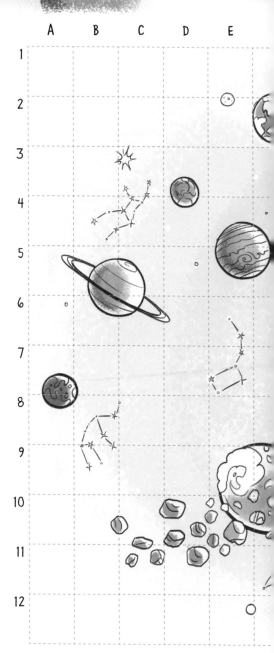

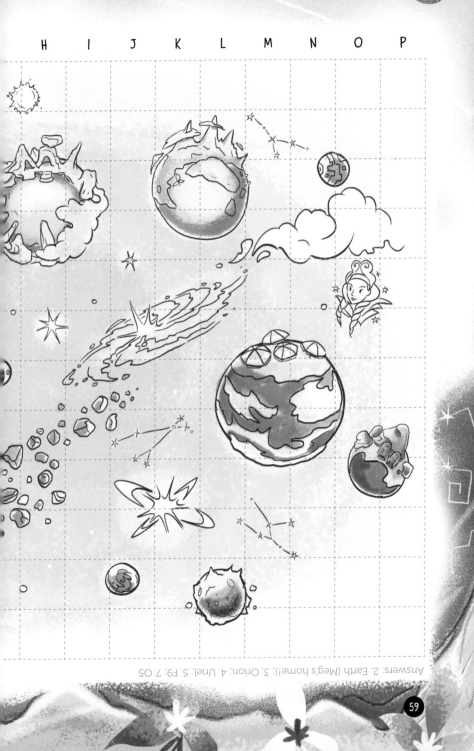

Clear the Cave

The Happy Medium doesn't like it when Meg, Charles Wallace, and Calvin walk around his cave because there are so many things they can knock over. Find a clear path for Meg and Calvin to walk to Charles Wallace.

Answer on page 140

What Kind of Scientist Are You?

Meg's parents are physicists, which is just one of the many different branches of science. Answer the questions below to learn more about what Meg's parents studied and to understand what kind of science is most interesting to you.

1. ON A CAMPING TRIP, YOU LOVE TO . . .

A   help start the campfire.

B   sleep under the stars.

C   search for plants and animals on a hike.

2. WHICH DIY PROJECT SOUNDS MOST INTERESTING TO YOU?

A   Paper airplane

B   Solar system mobile

C   Pressed flowers

3. TEACHERS SAY THAT YOU ARE . . .

A   a great problem solver.

B   very studious.

C   good at paying attention to details.

$E = h\nu = \frac{hc}{\lambda}$

$p = mv$

4. SOMEDAY YOU'D LIKE TO . . .

A go skydiving.

B watch a space shuttle launch.

C visit all the national parks.

5. IN A SCIENCE LAB, YOUR FAVORITE TOOL IS A . . .

A calculator.

B telescope.

C microscope.

6. ONE DAY YOU'D LIKE TO BE ABLE TO . . .

A solve large math problems in your head.

B recognize every constellation in the sky.

C identify every plant in the forest.

7. IF YOU WERE A FAMOUS SCIENTIST, YOU'D WANT TO BE KNOWN FOR . . .

A inventing a safe way to time travel.

B discovering alien life on a new planet.

C curing all diseases.

Answers on page 140

Earth Warrior Match-Up

Anyone can be an Earth Warrior—including you! According to the Mrs.'s, Earth Warriors are those who are willing to face darkness and bring their best work to light for the world. Match the warrior to their amazing work.

1. DR. JANE GOODALL

2. ABRAHAM LINCOLN

3. DR. MAYA ANGELOU

4. MAHATMA GANDHI

5. DR. MARIE CURIE

6. NELSON MANDELA

7. JANE AUSTEN

8. MEG MURRY

A First female to win the Nobel Prize, and the first person to win it twice.

B An African American poet and civil rights activist.

C A nonviolent activist who helped India gain independence from Britain.

D One of the best known female novelists from the eighteenth century.

E Scientist and conservation expert who studied and protected wild chimpanzees.

F One of the greatest American presidents and an opponent of slavery.

G Rescued renowned scientist Dr. Alex Murry from Camazotz.

H Former president of South Africa and supporter of peace and human rights.

Character Word Search

Circle the names of your favorite characters below.

```
A S L C O M N Q O W P P I K A L X R A B
Y F E O B V I I K M Z J A A G Y W I C E
Q I S J E R I C H F Z I O N I C H A H A
C L U R E F I X Y T O M A L O O P K A L
B A H H U O N M I A Q R L O W D A R R E
D I L O M R S W H A T S I T Z U M B L I
F F I V O T C H U T T W H R I M S R E D
Z A E H I I P U T S E H E E M O P B S A
D O L B O N E E B I N I M A K I N A W O
H I D X O B M U U R K C L P I N G O A S
G R I B Y R T Y N K O H M W O O T C L O
L O O T E A N Q S M G N F E L L I T L H
R R E A T S T U R S S Q O Z I N Y E A A
L O N W B X V F I S I O P M O R C H C E
H A P P Y M E D I U M T T R O W A L E S
S J O O K E G G E Y N W E S D E R N V O
E Q U N S G A A B Z O V I W O R T H C I
W E E G L X B F H I P X X H L L I C K E
N N O U R A A W P H L L O O H T C Y O P
A R E Q H O D K I I M W P L N X A Y Z E
```

CALVIN	HAPPY MEDIUM	MRS. WHICH
CHARLES WALLACE	MEG	MRS. WHO
FORTINBRAS	MRS. WHATSIT	VERONICA

Answers on page 140

SLAM DUNK!

Meg isn't great at basketball, but she's an all-star when it comes to math. Help her "slam dunk" her way through these problems.

$1 \times 7 =$ ___

$15 - 3 =$ ___

$8 + 7 =$ ___

$15 \div 3 =$ ___

$20 - 18 =$ ___

$3 + 4 =$ ___

$9 - 6 =$ ___

$20 \div 4 =$ ___

$6 \times 3 =$ ___

$12 - 6 =$ ___

$18 \div 9 =$ ___

$5 + 4 =$ ___

Now add all of the points together—what's your final score?
Answer: ___

Answers on page 140

Balancing Act

Meg can't seem to walk through the
Happy Medium's cave without toppling into
something! It doesn't take long before
he lectures her on the importance
of balance. Practice your balance
with the moves below.

1. Stand with your feet
together. Bend and
lift your left leg with
your knee facing
forward. Hold for 10
seconds. Repeat on
the right side.

2. Now do the same exercise but close your eyes while you're doing it. It's a lot harder to balance when your eyes are closed!

3. Now, keep your eyes closed and see if you can also raise your arms out to the side.

Design Your Own Creature

Aunt Beast comforts Meg after an especially rough tesser. The furry creature can't see or hear but she can feel, and she makes Meg feel loved. Design your own creature below.

WHAT IS YOUR CREATURE'S NAME?

_____

WHAT IS ITS SPECIAL TALENT?

_____

_____

_____

WHERE DOES IT LIVE?

_____

_____

_____

WHAT DOES IT LOOK LIKE? DRAW IT HERE.

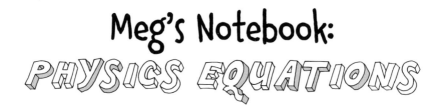

Meg's Notebook:
PHYSICS EQUATIONS

SPEED OF LIGHT:
299,792,458 meters per second
or 186,282 miles per second
or "c"

$E = mc^2$
Energy (E) = mass (m)
times the speed of
light (c) squared

$a = \Delta v / \Delta t$
acceleration (a) = change
(Δ) in velocity (v) divided
by change (Δ) in time (t)

MEG,
HAVE A GOOD DAY
AT SCHOOL! DON'T
FORGET TO PICK UP
CHARLES WALLACE.
XO,
MOM

NEWTON'S FIRST LAW:
An object at rest stays at rest; an object in motion stays in motion.

NEWTON'S SECOND LAW:
$$F = ma$$
Force (F) = mass (m) times acceleration (a)

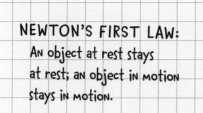

NEWTON'S THIRD LAW:
Every action has an equal and opposite reaction.

SIR ISSAC NEWTON
- Mathematician
- Physicist
- Astronomer
- Born in England
- Developed a theory of color
- Established laws of motion and gravity

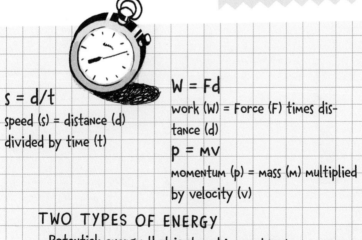

$$s = d/t$$
speed (s) = distance (d) divided by time (t)

$$W = Fd$$
work (W) = Force (F) times distance (d)

$$p = mv$$
momentum (p) = mass (m) multiplied by velocity (v)

TWO TYPES OF ENERGY
Potential: energy that is stored in an object
Kinetic: an object's energy resulting from its motion

MAGNIFYING GLASS

MICROSCOPE

CALCULATOR

BIOPHYSICS BOOK

NOTEBOOK

DNA MODEL

MICROSCOPE SLIDES

Answers on page 141

AWARD

Dr. Kate Murry's Laboratory

While Mr. Murry was missing, Mrs. Murry continued their research in hopes of finding him. Can you find the following objects in Mrs. Murry's disorganized lab so she can keep working on their tesseract theory?

Bustling Beach

Help Meg and Calvin save Charles Wallace from the mysterious man on the beach.

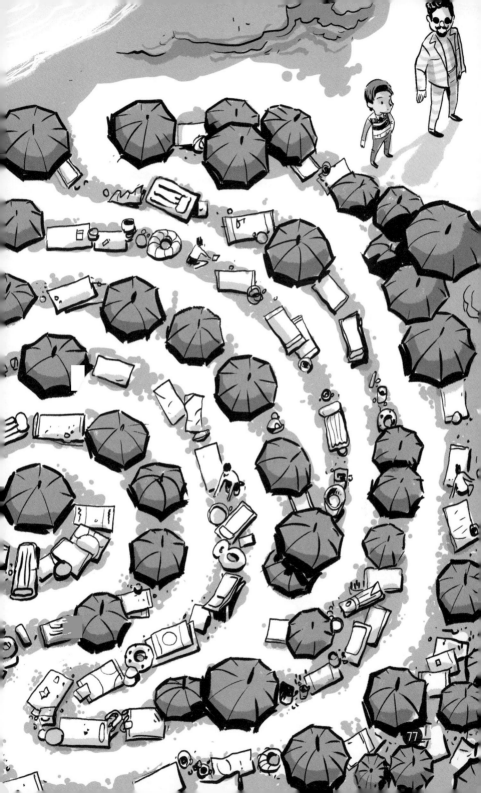

Connect the Dots

Draw a line from one number to the next to reveal
something unusual from Mrs. Who!

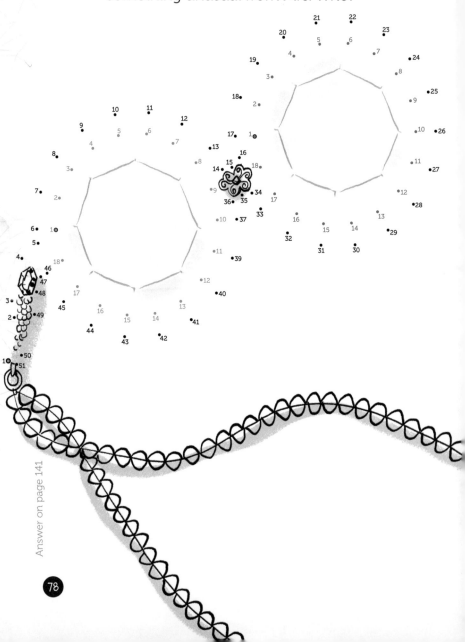

Which Is Bigger?

It's no wonder that Dr. Alex Murry is so hard to find once he tessers into the great unknown. The universe is so large, so old, so heavy, so hot, and so fast that scientists have had to come up with many different units of measurement just to capture these insanely large numbers. Draw a < or a > to show which is bigger, hotter, longer, or faster. The arrow should be pointing toward the smaller measurement.

100 days	◯	1,000 weeks
2 billion stars	◯	10 million stars
3 minutes	◯	90 seconds
1 year	◯	1 leap year
speed of sound	◯	speed of light
65 degrees Fahrenheit	◯	65 degrees Celsius
1 galactic year	◯	125 centuries
1 light-year	◯	750,000 miles
2 decades	◯	1 millennium
Sun's diameter	◯	Earth's diameter
5 trillion	◯	1 quintillion

Answers: 1. <; 2. >; 3. >; 4. <; 5. <; 6. >; 7. >; 8. <; 9. <; 10. >; 11. <

"Wild nights are my glory."

—Mrs. Whatsit

Mrs. Whatsit

Mrs. Whatsit calls Charles Wallace "prodigious," which means "impressively great." Using colored pencils or markers, design Mrs. Whatsit a prodigious outfit.

Scientist Name Scramble

These clues can help you unscramble the name of these famous scientists.

1.
BARTLE TINESINE
He came up with the equation $E = mc^2$.

_____

2.
SACIA NOWENT
He is the scientist who discovered gravity.

_____

3.
OLKINA SLATE
The radio and the X-ray are some of his inventions.

_____

4.
EARV IBNUR
Her calculations helped prove the existence of dark matter.

_____

5.
SMOHAT DINOSE
He invented the first electric lightbulb.

_____

6.
ERIAM ERICU
She discovered two elements: radium and polonium.

_____

7. NESTHEP WINGKAH
He's known for his groundbreaking research on blackholes in space.

_____

1. Albert Einstein; 2. Isaac Newton; 3. Nikola Tesla; 4. Vera Rubin, 5. Thomas Edison; 6. Marie Curie; 7. Stephen Hawking

BASKETBALL BREAKDOWN

The basketballs on Camazotz are all the same, but each of these balls is different—and a message is hidden within. Color each basketball to show the fraction or percentage given.

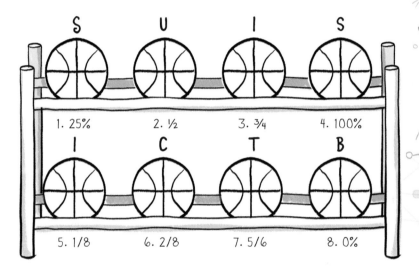

S	U	I	S
1. 25%	2. ½	3. ¾	4. 100%

I	C	T	B
5. 1/8	6. 2/8	7. 5/6	8. 0%

9. Write the letter on each ball from lowest to highest fraction or percentage to solve this riddle: What is Meg's nickname for Charles Wallace?

Which Mrs. Are You?

1. YOUR FRIENDS TURN TO YOU WHEN THEY'RE LOOKING FOR . . .

A   a good laugh.

B   random facts.

C   advice.

2. YOUR FAVORITE PART OF THE SCHOOL DAY IS WHEN YOU . . .

A   tell stories during lunch.

B   learn something you never knew before.

C   help a friend study for a test.

3. YOU'RE THE KIND OF PERSON WHO . . .

A   is friends with everyone.

B   stands out in a crowd.

C   is wise beyond your years.

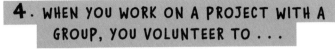

4. WHEN YOU WORK ON A PROJECT WITH A GROUP, YOU VOLUNTEER TO . . .

A present to the class.

B start the research.

C write up the final presentation.

5. IF YOU WERE AN ANIMAL, YOU WOULD BE A . . .

A dolphin.

B parrot.

C lion.

6. IF YOU COULD HAVE ONE MAGICAL POWER, YOU WOULD LOVE TO . . .

A fly.

B read people's minds.

C know the answer to everything.

7. IN YOUR BEDROOM, YOU HAVE . . .

A a karaoke machine.

B art supplies of all kinds.

C dozens and dozens of books.

Answers on page 141

Time

EARTH-BASED TIME TELLING

60 seconds = 1 minute

60 minutes = 1 hour or
3,600 seconds

24 hours = 1 day or
86,400 seconds

7 days = 1 week

14 days = 1 fortnight

1 year = 365 days, or
the time it takes Earth
to rotate on its axis

TIME ON OTHER PLANETS

1 Jupiter day = 10 hours

1 Saturn day = 11 hours

1 Neptune day = 16 hours

1 Uranus day = 17 hours

1 Earth day = 24 hours

1 Mars day = 25 hours

1 Mercury day = 1,408 hours

1 Venus day = 5,832 hours

SUN-BASED TIME TELLING

1 year = the time it takes a planet
to rotate around the Sun

olympiad = 4 years

lustrum = 5 years

indiction = 15 years

decade = 10 years

century = 100 years

millennium = 1,000 years

HOW OLD ARE YOU ON MARS?

You already know your age on Earth, but how old would you be on other planets? To figure it out, multiply your age by 365, then divide it by the number of Earth days that make up 1 year for each planet.

EXAMPLE:

Age on Mercury: 12 years old × 365 days = 4,380 Earth days ÷ 88 Earth days = 49.7 years old.

HOW MANY EARTH DAYS OLD ARE YOU?

Your age × 365 = Your age in Earth days

PLANET	EQUATION	AGE
Mercury	1 Mercury year = 88 Earth days	
Venus	1 Venus year = 225 Earth days	
Earth	1 Earth year = 365 Earth days	
Mars	1 Mars year = 687 Earth days	
Jupiter	1 Jupiter year = 4,333 Earth days	
Saturn	1 Saturn year = 10,759 Earth days	
Uranus	1 Uranus year = 30,685 Earth days	
Neptune	1 Neptune year = 60,182 Earth days	

Create Your Own Quote

Mrs. Who loves to speak in quotations. She quotes famous lines from historical figures like the Buddha, Helen Keller, and Shakespeare. But at one point, she finally speaks her own truth: "We are our light and our dark, made whole by our love."

Write a quote below that summarizes what you think is most important in your life right now, and what you believe to be true no matter what.

Planet Word Search

Can you find the planet names hidden below?

```
C R D S A E H J K A D X Z G B D P X X T
Z W E M K L Z E E T A D G X T O P S Z Q
Q A A Z V N K M O U D K L D W R P K B F
V B J K H C C R H D J O Y F B K L J J H
B F E Y E A R T H V V B M L G F D H K U
X L X Z Q M R Y U U I P J V D H M A R S
G J K F B A M K L V F J U F J K L I G L
A A D G O Z M F D H N E P T U N E R U O
O P R Y N O F J I T G J I R U L F J K L
B F R S A T U R N R H J T T S V Q V G H
T U O P H Z F U I R B M E T J J E N M R
N G F D H K M B F T Y O R I O N V N Z X
Y J K M B G M L D L N B V F U N K L H M
R Y U I O P V M H J J K L S V F N M G B
Y U I I X C H E L B M Z D B T E N K B F
O O C B N K P R F B B F E Q F V N J I K
V B N J G V N C H K K G C B N M K U T B
F G E B N K K U R A N U S C F T H I S B
G F H J K H N R V N M M B M Q D G K E Q
R Q U O M V Z Y F H J Y V Z W M V N U M
```

CAMAZOTZ   JUPITER   NEPTUNE   URANUS
EARTH   MARS   ORION   URIEL
IXCHEL   MERCURY   SATURN   VENUS

Answers on page 142

Star Chart

These are some of the most famous constellations in the night sky. Did you know that it's impossible to see every constellation at the same time? Someone standing at the North Pole would see very different constellations from someone standing at the South Pole. Your view also depends on the time of year— as the Earth orbits the Sun, your view of the stars changes, too.

URSA MAJOR A.K.A. BIG DIPPER

CASSIOPEIA

URSA MINOR A.K.A. LITTLE DIPPER

GEMINI

TAURUS

ARIES

LEO

ORION

PISC

EAST

CANIS MAJOR

NORTH

VEGA

LYRA

CYGNUS

EQUATOR WEST

AQUILA

AQUARIUS

SCORPIUS

SOUTH

91

RAINBOW GLASSES

Mrs. Who's glasses are quite unusual—they are made of prisms! Did you know that prisms can create rainbows? White (visible) light goes in on one side and many colors come out on the other side.

HOW?

When white light enters a prism, it separates into different wavelengths (and colors!) of light. Each angle produces a different color of light.

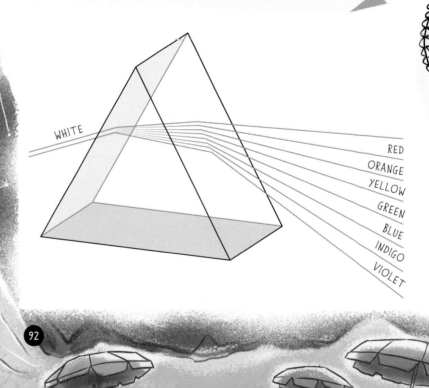

WHITE

RED
ORANGE
YELLOW
GREEN
BLUE
INDIGO
VIOLET

Color in each line as noted.

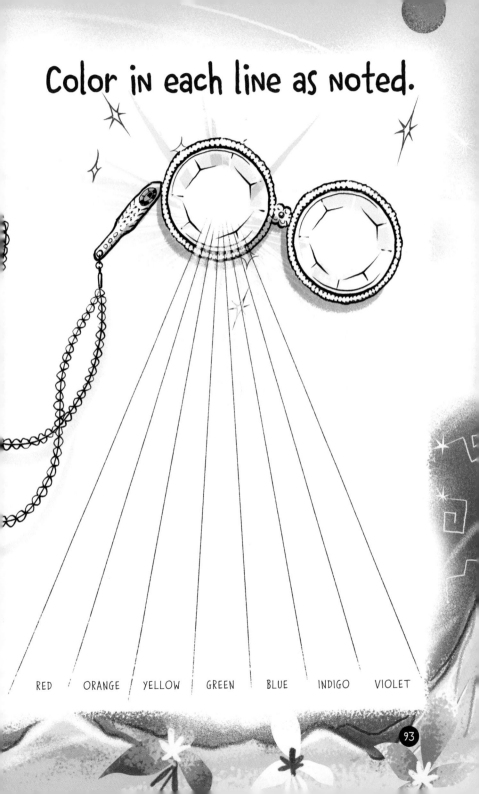

RED   ORANGE   YELLOW   GREEN   BLUE   INDIGO   VIOLET

Galaxy Search

The universe is a large place. According to Dr. Alex Murry, there could be 200 billion galaxies that stretch across 91 billion light years. Can you find the items shown on the right in this illustration?

CAMAZOTZ

EARTH

IXCHEL

MOON

MRS. WHATSIT

NORTH STAR

ORION

SATURN

SHOOTING STAR

URSA MINOR

Answers on page 142

To Tesser or Not to Tesser

See how well you understand the rules of tessering by answering these multiple-choice questions.

1. A TESSERACT IS FOUND IN THE ___ DIMENSION.

A   fifth

B   eighth

C   third

2. TO FEEL BETTER AFTER TESSERING, GET A . . .

A   quote from Mrs. Who.

B   glass of warm milk.

C   hug from Aunt Beast.

3. DR. MURRY BELIEVES LIGHT AND ___ VIBRATE AT THE SAME FREQUENCY.

A   darkness

B   love

C   the moon

4. MEG DEMONSTRATES HOW A TESSERACT WORKS WITH . . .

A a dog toy shaped like an ant and a piece of string.

B dog and a leash.

C milk and cookies.

5. WHICH CHARACTER HAS THE HARDEST TIME TESSERING?

A Charles Wallace

B Calvin

C Meg

6. DR. ALEX MURRY SAYS THE FIFTH DIMENSION IS OUTSIDE THE RULES OF . . .

A lightness and darkness.

B yesterday and tomorrow.

C time and space.

7. TO TESSER, YOU MUST BE AT ONE WITH THE UNIVERSE AND WITH YOUR . . .

A dreams.

B self.

C anger.

Answers: 1. A; 2. C; 3. B; 4. A; 5. C; 6. C; 7. B

The Mrs.'s Agree

In darkness there is still light. Find the
constellations hidden within the night
sky of this dot-to-dot puzzle.

Answers on page 142

Be
brave.
Be
bold.
Be
free.

YOU-NIQUE!

Meg has trouble tessering as easily as everyone else. To tesser correctly, you must want to return to yourself at the end of each journey. What do you love about yourself? What makes you different?

Big Books

Charles Wallace may be young, but he reads a lot.
Find out how much by solving the equations below.

1. On his bookshelf, Charles Wallace has 10 books. He's read 7 of them. What percentage of books has he not read?

2. If each of the 7 books Charles Wallace has read has 500 pages, and each page has 250 words, how many words has Charles Wallace read?

3. Which book has more words: a book with 1,000 pages and 200 words per page, or a book with 800 pages and 250 words per page?

4. Charles Wallace wants Calvin to read him a book that has fewer than 1,000 pages. If *Ulysses* by James Joyce has 265,000 words and there are about 250 words per page, will Calvin read it aloud?

5. If Charles Wallace wants to read *The Complete Works of William Shakespeare*, which has 2,000 pages, and it takes him 2 hours to read 100 pages, how many hours will it take him to read the book?

Answers on page 142

FIND THE DIFFERENCES: ORION

The Happy Medium lives inside
a dark cave on Orion. Look closely
to find the 10 differences
between the illustrations.
Circle them all!

Answers on page 142

Design Your Own Mrs.

Everyone is unique in their own way, but each of
the Mrs.'s has an especially unusual personality
and talents. Create a friend of Mrs. Who,
Mrs. Which, and Mrs. Whatsit.

What's her name?

_____

_____

_____

What are her talents?

_____

_____

_____

What planet is she from?

_____

_____

_____

What does she look like?

_____

_____

_____

_____

_____

_____

Draw your Mrs. here.

Reveal the Future

The Happy Medium is known for his visions.
Help Meg uncover his vision by using the
key to reveal the coded message below.

___ ___ ___

___ ___ ___ ___

___ ___ ___ ___

___ ___ ___ ___ ___ ___ ___

Answer: You find your balance

Trivia Crossword

The anwsers to these clues will help you fill in this crossword puzzle.

Across

1. Evil energy that is taking over the world. (2 words)

2. Dr. Alex Murry says light and _____ vibrate at the same frequency.

3. The planet on which Dr. Alex Murry is trapped.

4. *A _____ in Time.*

5. "It was a _____ and stormy night."

6. Meg's dog.

7. She speaks in quotes. (2 words)

Down

8. How Meg time travels.

9. Meg's neighbor.

10. He lives on Orion. (2 words)

11. The fourth dimension.

Answers on page 142

Super Stars!

How much do you know about the glowing balls of gas that light our sky? Some of the following statements are true and some are false. Guess which is which!

		TRUE	FALSE
1.	The Sun is the closest star to Earth.	✓	☐
2.	Among other colors, stars can be red, white, or blue.	✓	☐
3.	The hottest stars are red.	☐	✓
4.	Some stars are more than 1,000 times larger than the Sun.	✓	☐
5.	Stars never burn out.	☐	✓
6.	There are hundreds of billions of stars in the Milky Way.	✓	☐

Answers: 1. T, 2. T, 3. F, 4. T, 5. F, 6. T

Elements
Word Search

Elements are the building blocks that create everything in our universe. There are 118 elements, but this word search only has 15 of them. See if you can find them all!

```
A C D W D B B H J D S M Z G I E M I Q D
B F K T H I C Y A B F Y M B C X T P U W
I M P B Y D K D X A S J T C I J V N X I
X W C F C F A R T T W R P D K Q H R H A
K Y H F X E H O C A Y X P S N R E H U J
X B Z P T T H G U G V M Q L G O L D B K
I X L T H I B E W L X C H C N Y I A X H
X C X M B C J N J S E K B A X P U E S I
H D A G W O O D P O T A S S I U M Z P X
A W L Y F P D K L Y S S D Y A H C S S T
I H B S X P R X U W I L F Z O P E D B M
X O P W B E E W T H B X J N U D U G N I
H K O U W R A D O N N O I D M W S E G C
Q P Z S X A A P N S W D W S T S G G P X
X I B U M P B C I P T X M I P Y M H G J
W M L T T H I U U C J Y P S X A C A B H
A P B H C S H R M N I T R O G E N M V W
Y X U L I T H I U M R P A O F K N V K X
P H U F P C M U P S O Y O U N N E O N F
X I J W A M B M I B N M B X I L I A N Y
```

COPPER   HELIUM   LEAD   NITROGEN   POTASSIUM
CURIUM   HYDROGEN   LITHIUM   OXYGEN   RADON
GOLD   IRON   NEON   PLUTONIUM   XENON

Answers on page 143

Color-In Puzzle

Mrs. Whatsit says that flowers are the universe's best gossipers. But the flowers of Uriel don't speak English—they speak colors. Each letter represents a color in this illustration. Follow the code to reveal the image and a special message.

A = YELLOW, B = PINK, C = ORANGE, D = GREEN, E = BLUE

Answers on page 143

Hug Helper

Meg goes through a lot in trying to save her dad. She really needs a hug to feel better! Help her reach Aunt Beast as quickly as possible by finding the fastest way through this maze.

Answer on page 143

"'To be SURPRISED, to WONDER, is to begin to UNDERSTAND."

Gasset, Spanish."
—Mrs. Who

What Do You Love?

As Charles Wallace says, it's hard to be good at something you don't love. Meg happens to love science, and that's why she's great at cracking equations and calculations on the fly. What makes you happy? Write those things below in a list.

1. _____
_____

2. _____
_____

3. _____
_____

4. _____
_____

5. _____
_____

Word of the Day

Charles Wallace loves learning a new definition every day. Match these words with their definitions, then try to use them in the sentences below.

1. Exclusive

2. Luminous

3. Exaltation

4. Home

5. Prodigious

6. Aberration

7. Seer

A Extreme happiness.

B The place where one lives.

C Deviation from what is normal or expected.

D Restricted or limited to.

E A person who envisions the future.

F Bright or shining.

G Especially great or large.

sleep

118

shining

Now use the vocabulary words above to fill in these blanks.

1. Meg can't wait to get _____ and sleep in her own bed.

2. Charles Wallace usually get As in school, so a C is an _____.

3. Time travel is _____ to only the people who know how to tesser.

4. Sometimes Mrs. Which is normal-sized and other times she is _____.

5. Stars may look dim from Earth, but up close they are _____.

6. When Dr. Alex Murry returned home he was in a state of _____.

prodigious
happiness
home
exaltation
luminous
travel
star
time
exclusive

Answers: 1. Home; 2. Aberration; 3. Exclusive; 4. Prodigious; 5. Luminous; 6. Exaltation.

FIND the DiFFeReNces: CAMAZotz

Meg, Calvin, and Charles Wallace run into a neighborhood on Camazotz where everything and everyone look exactly the same. But if you're a keen observer, you can find 10 differences. Circle them all!

Answers on page 143

Which Kind of Earth Warrior Are You?

There have been many famous Earth Warriors throughout history. See which one you are most like by answering the following questions.

1. AT SCHOOL YOU'RE KNOWN FOR . . .

 asking interesting questions.

B being kind to everyone.

© your creativity.

2. YOUR FAVORITE SUBJECT IN SCHOOL IS . . .

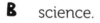 math.

B science.

© English.

3. YOU COULDN'T IMAGINE A DAY WITHOUT . . .

 learning something new.

B hugging your favorite pet.

© listening to music.

4. YOUR PERFECT DAY WOULD BE SPENT . . .

A   at the library reading anything you wanted to read.

B   outside with friends in a park.

C   with a blank notebook and a freshly sharpened pencil.

5. YOU'RE REALLY GOOD AT MEMORIZING . . .

A   interesting facts.

B   your friends' birthdays.

C   the lyrics to songs.

6. ONE DAY YOU'D LIKE TO BE ABLE TO . . .

A   tutor other students.

B   adopt a pet.

C   paint a mural.

7. IN THE FUTURE, IT'S IMPORTANT THAT . . .

A   every kid gets a good education.

B   we protect endangered species.

C   we respect each other's opinions.

Answers on page 144

Magic Trick: Coin Jump

You might not be able to tesser to another planet in the blink of an eye just yet, but you can do a magic trick that makes it seem possible! In this trick, you'll make it look like a coin magically jumps instantly from one hand to the other. Here's how it works.

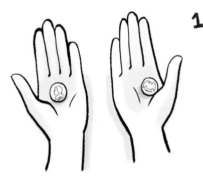

1. Place a quarter in the palm of each hand. The quarter in your left hand should be in the center of your palm. The quarter in your right hand should be near your thumb.

2. Quickly flip both hands over and slap them onto the table. As you're flipping your hands over, flick the coin in your right hand under your left hand. (This might take practice!)

3. Ask your audience, "Where do you think the coins are?" They'll probably answer, "One under each hand."

KEEP PRACTICING!

The faster you flip your hands—and the farther the coin in your hand is located from the center of the palm—the better the trick will look.

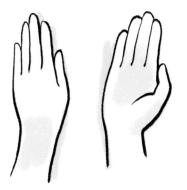

4. Reveal your empty right hand palm up. Now reveal the two coins in your left hand. Ta-da!

Scientific Breakthroughs

In *A Wrinkle in Time*, Doctors Kate and Alex Murry's research on tessering led to a major scientific discovery. Number the life-changing inventions below from past to present. Write "1" under the oldest invention, and "10" under the newest invention.

_____   _____   _____

_____   _____

_____   _____   _____

_____   _____

Answers on page 144

Puzzling Equations

One plus two equals three, but does a flower plus a flower equal a tree? Help Meg solve these visual math puzzles.

1.

$12 + \heartsuit = 15$

$10 - \heartsuit = 7$

$\heartsuit - 2 = 1$

$\heartsuit = \underline{\hspace{2cm}}$

2.

$\text{flower} + \text{flower} = 20$

$\text{flower} - \text{tree} = 3$

$\text{tree} = \underline{\hspace{2cm}}$

3.

$\text{sun} + \text{sun} = \text{star} + 2$

$\text{sun} + 4 = \text{star}$

$\text{star} = \underline{\hspace{2cm}}$

4.

$\text{dog} \times \text{dog} + 1 = 10$

$\text{dog} \times \text{cat} \times \text{cat} = 12$

$\text{dog} - \text{cat} = \underline{\hspace{2cm}}$

5.

$\text{book} \times \text{book} = \text{glasses} + 9$

$\text{book} + 11 = \text{glasses}$

$\text{glasses} = \underline{\hspace{2cm}}$

Flower Crossword

The flowers may speak in colors, but they are filled with knowledge. Glean some of their wisdom by using the clues below to fill in this crossword puzzle.

Down

1. Find the _____ Medium.

2. You must be a _____ for Earth.

3. Meg must use her _____.

4. You can _____ the answers, but you can't avoid them.

5. Wild _____ are Mrs. Whatsit's glory.

6. Trust the _____ that's around you.

Across

7. You must not be afraid to be _____.

8. In darkness, there is still _____.

9. Flowers are the universe's best _____.

10. The only thing that travels faster than light is _____.

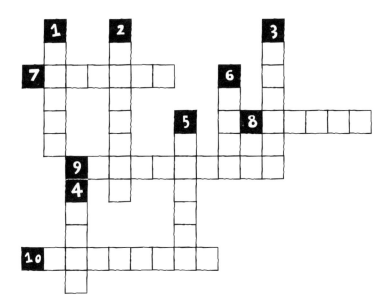

Answers on page 144

Origami Heart

Meg's origami enfolder conceals a hidden heart. Make your own origami heart by following these directions. You'll need a square sheet of origami paper to start or a piece of thin paper cut into an 8" × 8" square.

1. Start with a square oriented like a diamond.

2. Fold the square in half, top corner to bottom corner. Crease, then unfold.

3. Fold the square in half, left corner to right corner. Crease, then unfold.

4.

Fold the top corner to the center.

5.

Fold the bottom corner upward to the top edge.

6.

Fold the left and right bottom corners to the top center crease.

7.

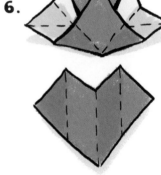

Smooth the edges by folding the tips of the top and side corners backward.

Time Tellers

Length, width, and height are the first three dimensions. Use the key below to crack the code. It has something to do with the fourth dimension . . .

I = 1:30

N = 3:15

U = 9:00

E = 6:45

T = 11:45   F = 10:30   H = 4:15

Tesser Back to Earth

Help Meg and her father find their way back from Camazotz to Earth.

Answer on page 144

TO BE OUR WARRIORS FOR EARTH."

—Mrs. Which

Answer Key

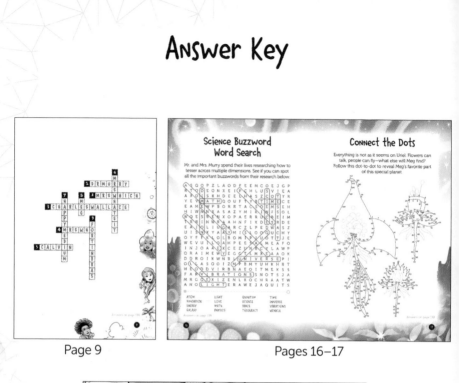

Page 9

Pages 16–17

Pages 28–29

If you answered mostly A's, you're more of a Charles Wallace!

You're friendly and a good student, just like Charles Wallace. You get along with everyone because you're an interesting person who genuinely wants to help. Maybe you haven't read *The Complete Works of William Shakespeare*—yet!—but you'd like to someday. You love gaining knowledge and sharing it with others.

If you answered mostly B's, you're more of a Meg!

When you put your mind to something, you succeed, just like Meg. You're a little harder to get to know when it comes to meeting new friends or strangers, but you're very loyal to the people in your life. Just because you're quiet doesn't mean you don't care. In fact, you are a very kind person!

Pages 32–33

Pages 34–35

Page 43

Page 48

Answers:

1. 12 hours × 8 quotes = 96 quotes per day

2. If 1 hour = 60 minutes, and 2 tessers × 10 minutes per tesser = 20 minutes, then 60 minutes − 20 minutes = 40 minutes

3. 105 feet − 5 feet = 100 feet; 100 feet × 12 inches = 1,200 inches

Page 57

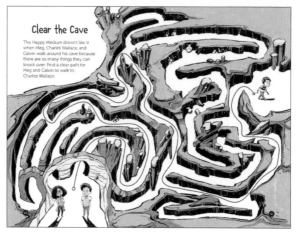

Pages 60–61

If you picked mostly A's, you're a physicist!

Physicists, like Meg's parents, study everything from the tiniest of atoms to the entire universe! They're very good problem solvers who use mathematical equations to explain theories. Isaac Newton and Albert Einstein were famous physicists.

If you picked mostly B's, you're an astronomer!

If you love space, you'll love astronomy. Astronomers study stars, planets, and galaxies. They sometimes gaze through telescopes, but are often found researching and analyzing data. Galileo and Vera Rubin were famous astronomers.

If you picked mostly C's, you're a biologist!

At the most basic level, biologists study life. That may mean looking at tiny cells under a microscope, at fish in the sea, or at plants in the wild. Charles Darwin was a famous biologist, as is Jane Goodall.

Pages 62–63

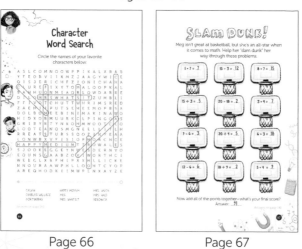

Page 66   Page 67

Pages 74–75

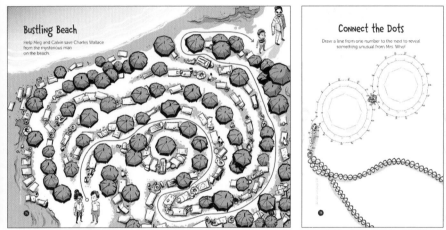

Pages 76–77

Page 78

If you picked mostly A's, you're Mrs. Whatsit!

Mrs. Whatsit is spunky, friendly, outgoing, and fun. You're not afraid to be the center of attention. You love to be around friends and make them laugh with silly stories—and they love it, too!

If you picked mostly B's, you're Mrs. Who!

Mrs. Who is creative, interesting, and smart. Like you, she may not speak all the time, but when she does, everyone listens. And you always listen to those around you. You're a great friend and student.

If you picked mostly C's, you're Mrs. Which!

Mrs. Which is wise and all-knowing. Just like Mrs. Which, you have a way of understanding your friends' thoughts and feelings. They turn to you for advice and always know they can rely on you.

Pages 84–85

Page 89

Pages 94–95

Page 98

Answers:

1. 7/10 = 70%. He has not read 30% of the books.

2. 7 × 500 = 3,500. 3,500 × 250 = 875,000 words.

3. 1,000 × 200 = 200,000 words; 800 × 250 = 200,000 words. They're the same length.

4. 265,000 ÷ 250 = 1,060 pages. No, Calvin will not read it aloud.

5. 2,000 ÷ 100 = 20. 20 × 2 = 40 hours.

Page 101

Page 102

Page 109

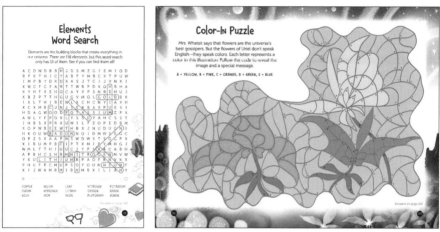

Page 111

Pages 112–113

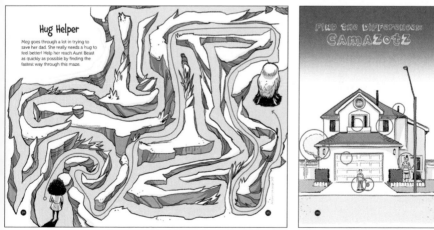

Pages 114–115

Page 120

If you picked mostly A's, you're Albert Einstein!

Say the name Einstein and one word comes to mind—genius! Albert Einstein is known for being a professor, winning the Nobel Prize in physics, and discovering his famous theory, $E = mc^2$. It takes years of intense studying and research to become so smart, but you're not afraid of hard work. A strong mind will take you far!

If you picked mostly B's, you're Jane Goodall!

Jane Goodall is a famous primatologist who studied chimpanzees. She also believes in protecting animals and the environment. If you love animals and the environment, there are many things you can do to help, such as recycling, biking to school instead of being driven there, or volunteering at an animal shelter.

If you picked mostly C's, you're Maya Angelou!

Maya Angelou was a famous poet and activist. She knew words are important and stories are powerful. Because you are creative, you could also use your artistic side to make a difference, be it through writing, drawing, or singing.

Pages 122–123

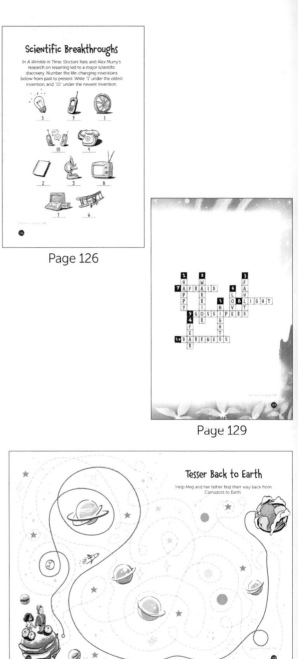

Page 126

Page 129

Pages 134–135

The Cook's Family

To Marcelo, Ron, Mel,
Joyce, Elizabeth, Patrick, Jimmy and
all the others who helped with
the workshops of *Dragonwings*.

CONTENTS

O N E

The Celestial Forest

When the fat man plunged out of the restaurant onto the pavement, I could have dodged. But then he would have broadsided my grandmother. So I prepared myself to take the charge like a basketball player. Ms. Grant, my P.E. teacher, would have been proud of the way I stood my ground.

He was big—weighing maybe two hundred pounds—and shouting things over his shoulder, so he never saw me. I got ready to be steamrollered, but it was Grandmother who came to my rescue.

One of her canes shot over my shoulder. Its brass tip struck the fat man in the chest as neatly as a cue stick hitting an eight-ball. In fact, the man even bounced back a pace.

"Watch where you're going!" Grandmother snapped. "You don't own the sidewalk." She spoke with a trace of a British accent that she had picked up in Hong Kong, where she had lived most of her life.

The big man turned to face us in surprise. "Hey," he said, rubbing his chest. But before he could say anything more, a flood of angry Chinese swept him past us and down the sidewalk. The restaurant looked like a bottle of Coca-Cola that someone had shaken up— only it was people bubbling out instead of foam. Grandmother nimbly reversed her cane and hooked the handle around my arm, pulling me to the side, where she had already stepped.

"I could never take you to Hong Kong, Robin," she muttered. "You'd get trampled in a minute."

The fat man was carried away on the river of humanity fleeing the restaurant. Its front was painted a garish yellow. Overhead there was a sign. At the top were red Chinese characters and beneath them were English words: The Celestial Forest. At the bottom of the sign were cartoon-like sketches of trees seen through a moon gate.

There was an old paper menu taped to the big plate glass window. The only thing in English was the prices, all of which seemed low, even for Chinatown. Inside, I saw that the restaurant was small with only about a dozen Formica tables and cheap wooden chairs.

A man in a white shirt and bow tie pursued the fugitives outside. He was waving a green order pad in his hand. "Come back here," he called indignantly. "You already placed your order."

A man in a gray suit turned around. "I've been waiting an hour," he declared in English. "Get that lazy Wolf to work. And if he won't work, fire him. That's how you run a business."

The waiter waved his order pad forlornly. "Come back. He'll be fine in a minute."

He seemed so heartbroken I couldn't help feeling sorry for him, and because everyone else had spoken in English, I did the same, "Are you all right?"

The waiter raised his head, and I figured he was about sixty, Grandmother's age, but small pouches beneath his eyes gave him a sleepy look.

As often happened in Chinatown, he ignored me. Instead, he gazed at Grandmother. "You'd be about the right age," he said.

Grandmother shifted uncomfortably. "For what?"

The waiter was staring at Grandmother's shoes and her canes. Suddenly he grew excited. "And you'd be the right type."

Had her stance given away the fact that her feet were crippled? Grandmother balanced her weight now on just one cane so she could use the other as a weapon. "What do you mean by that? I'll show you what I'm good for."

The waiter crouched, holding up his arms protectively. Because of the tourists passing by, he switched to Chinese. "My friend is the cook. He misses his family so much all he can do is sit and cry. In the meantime, our customers starve."

"Maybe if he called his family on the telephone," I suggested.

The waiter hesitated and looked around nervously, as if he were afraid of being overheard. Then he turned back to Grandmother. "They're dead," he said finally. "So couldn't you pretend to be his wife?"

Grandmother lifted her cane and poked the waiter in the chest. "Don't be silly."

The waiter leaned against the cane and spoke frantically. "He really just needs someone to talk to. Just for a few minutes."

Grandmother shoved harder on her cane. "Go away before I call the police."

"I'll pay," the waiter said and a moment later added, "And you'll get free meals." He started to reach into his pocket.

Through the window, I could see the restaurant was almost empty. And the few people there were putting on their coats as if they were getting ready to leave, too.

The waiter seemed so anxious that I pitied him. And how awful for the cook. What if he lost his job? "Couldn't we talk to him for just a few minutes?" I asked Grandmother.

Grandmother turned on me. "It simply isn't done. We can't pretend to be his family."

"But my friends and I pretend all the time in dance," I argued, as much for myself as for her. "Sometimes I'm a butterfly. Sometimes a swan. What's the harm in it?"

"When you're desperate enough, you'll believe anything," the waiter coaxed. "And if he doesn't, you're free to go."

Grandmother shook her head. "What would your mother say? The man sounds crazy."

I wasn't sure, either, but with Grandmother along, I felt safe enough not only to observe a wolf but to walk straight into his den. "We'd be doing a kindness for a lonely old man."

"Well, I don't know . . ." Grandmother hesitated.

The waiter seized his opportunity. Grabbing Grandmother by the arm, he yanked the door open. "There you are," he announced loudly. "Your husband's been wondering where you are." And he pulled my grandmother right inside and across the worn, red linoleum.

I chased him through the doorway. "Hey! Let go of her!"

But the waiter was already yelling toward the kitchen. "Hey, Wolf, your wife is here."

A man of medium height in a T-shirt and apron emerged. "Who's here?"

"Why, your wife, of course."

"My what?" As Wolf approached us, I could see that his mouth and eyes were small, giving him a boyish appearance—although his hair was gray. In his hand was the biggest cleaver I had ever seen. It was as big as a machete. His sleeves had been rolled back to expose forearms as bloody as the blade.

I would have bolted for the street, but I knew Grandmother couldn't move very fast. I couldn't abandon her, so I took her arm instead.

Wolf studied Grandmother for a long time with the saddest eyes I had ever seen. His gaze lingered longest on her canes and her feet, but he didn't say anything. It was as if both of them were afraid to be the first to speak.

Then he saw me clutching Grandmother. "Who are you?" Wolf asked. When he leaned toward us, I could smell liquor on his breath.

I stood frozen, afraid of saying something that might make him use the cleaver on me. It had been easy to talk about acts of mercy. It was quite the opposite to face the real thing. Maybe Grandmother had been right.

As his stare deepened, it occurred to me that our silence also might anger him. It took me a couple of tries before I found my voice. "Your granddaughter," I said in Chinese.

The waiter seemed just as surprised as Wolf that I could speak Chinese. Wolf gazed at me. Well, I had to admit that I didn't look the part. I had brown hair and green eyes, and looked more like my American father than my Chinese mother.

Whenever I went to Chinatown I felt as if I wasn't a real member of an exclusive club. I used to find excuses not to go, but this time I hadn't been able to get out of escorting Grandmother.

"I don't have a granddaughter," Wolf said.

The waiter seized the moment. "She means your daughter. I still think she speaks pretty good."

"Don't you recognize me, Father?" I asked.

"Father" was the magical word. Suddenly, Wolf became very interested. It was like watching a marionette whose strings had finally been picked up. His back straightened; his head lifted.

When you were small, did you ever go over to a new friend's house and play dolls? You would start by saying, "Let's pretend this doll is the father . . ." and so on. And when you were done spinning out your fantasy, you could only wait for your new friend to pick up her cue—or not. Maybe she had her own ideas of what to do. And that would bring your fantasy crashing down.

Or sometimes when my friends and I were improvising a dance at Leah's. And I would be trying to move as a bird, wondering if the others would pick up on my idea and fly with me.

Wolf's eyes said he knew quite well it was a game. "Come into the kitchen," he said.

TWO

The Cook's Family

The kitchen wasn't what I expected. I thought it would be full of cockroaches running over greasy walls, but instead every surface was clean and neat. Twin fluorescent tubes overhead cast a relentless, bright light on everything below. The ceiling and walls had been painted a glossy light yellow so the light broke into tiny lightning-like zigzags all around. And the black-and-white checkerboard linoleum floor looked worn but freshly mopped.

On tables were huge platters of uncooked, stuffed wontons, like pyramids of slick miniature turbans. Vegetables were sliced, diced, and prepared any other way you could. And the air was thick with the smells of hot oil and chopped garlic. But the huge woks on the stoves sat empty.

In the corner, by a big metal sink, was a man in a stained apron, looking at us in fright. He was in his thirties and had discolored teeth. I figured he was a dishwasher because he wore rubber gloves the size of catcher's mitts on his hands.

Wolf moved to the opposite corner, toward the stove, where an empty liquor bottle sat among his utensils. Raising the cleaver, he slammed it into a slab of meat on a big wooden board. Years of use had worn a groove down the middle. To my immense relief, I finally realized that the blood on his knife and arms belonged to a piece of beef.

Leaving the cleaver in the meat, he faced us again, the corners of his mouth twitching up in a smile. It wasn't the grin of a crazy man. It was the expression of a man who was amused. "Are you studying hard?" he asked me.

In the meantime, the waiter had sidled in and dug his elbow into my side.

"Yes," I mumbled.

When the waiter coughed loudly, I added, "Father." It made me feel suddenly disloyal to Dad.

"Good." He wiped his bloody hands on a towel. "Have you learned to write?" It was hard to say if it was a statement or a question.

With more confidence I shook my head. "Not yet."

Wolf turned to grandmother with the same teasing tone. "How come *you* don't write me then?"

It's a hard thing to be in a play for which no one has a script. The waiter's eyes widened in panic.

"You didn't get our letters?" I ad-libbed.

"No," Wolf said.

"Mother wrote and wrote," I said.

"Then I owe you an apology." Wolf bowed to Grandmother.

The waiter leaned over conspiratorially and whispered out of the side of his mouth. "You're doing just great, but get him to cook now."

I plucked the nearest green slip hanging from a steel clip near my head. On it were Chinese characters written in a jagged hand. "Father, what's this?"

"Don't play with those," Wolf said and snatched it from me. "This is very important." Glancing down at it, he put it back. Then he went to the biggest rice cooker I had ever seen—it looked as if it held a couple of gallons. Lifting the lid, he grabbed a big spoon and dumped huge amounts of rice on a plate.

Grandmother cleared her throat. "How . . . how are you?" she asked Wolf in Chinese.

As Wolf glanced at the slip of green paper, the waiter said, "Those people are still here, but not these." And he began to pull away some of the receipts.

Wolf tossed handfuls of cut chicken and vegetables into a wok. As soon as they hit the hot metal sides, they began to sizzle. A moment later, he added a dipper full of black bean sauce. The resulting smells made my mouth water.

"Fine," he said after slow deliberation. "How are you?"

"Good," Grandmother said, and then because she could think of nothing else, she added, "It's sunny today."

"It's always sunny in Chinatown," Wolf said as he put spoonfuls of chicken and vegetables beside the rice.

I almost said something about it being foggy out where we lived, but I caught myself. I was supposed to be his daughter, after all. Instead, I said, "It's a shame to be cooped up inside on such a nice day."

He placed the plate on a ledge. "But I love my kitchen now that you're both here." Lifting his head, he began to sing in a quavery but pleasant voice,

"I love a lady far away.
She never eats. She pines all day.
When she's asleep, she dreams of me—
The man who lives across the sea."

It was a pleasant tune, and when I heard the line about a sleeping woman, I thought of Aurora, the Sleeping Beauty. I was playing the part of Red Riding Hood in an excerpt from *Sleeping Beauty* when lots of fairy-tale characters entertain at the wedding.

Next to me, Grandmother sighed. "I haven't heard that song in a long time."

"Everyone used to sing it." He began to put slices of beef and ginger into another wok.

"Yes, that one spring," Grandmother agreed. There

was a soft, dreamy smile on her face that made her look years younger.

Wolf smiled now that they had found more familiar ground. "And butterfly earrings were all the fashion." It didn't take long for the thinly sliced beef to cook, and soon he was ladling the ginger beef onto another plate of rice that the waiter had prepared.

I opened the swinging door for the waiter as he hustled out of the kitchen, balancing the pot and plates. Ironic cheers came from the dining room, but in the kitchen we ignored the sound. Over in his corner, the dishwasher had begun to clean the old dishes with a huge spraying device.

Grandmother looked around for something to sit on, and then, when she saw nothing, she leaned against the doorframe. "I wanted butterfly earrings so badly, but we were too poor."

Wolf took up another green slip and read the order. "I always meant to buy her . . ." He corrected himself hastily, "I mean, I always meant to buy a pair for you."

I had been dreading having to talk about family and his home village—details that we didn't know. However, Grandmother and he spoke more about the old days back in China when they were both young.

I went to get a spare chair from the dining room, and when I brought it back into the kitchen, Grandmother sat down gratefully. At the stove, Wolf began to sing,

"Let's trade places, Madame Moon,
So I can see her very soon.
I'll touch her tears with my bright light
And make them pearls for her delight."

Grandmother shifted self-consciously. "I don't re-member those lyrics, though."

Wolf dashed some oil from a bottle into a wok. Im-mediately it began to sizzle and make sharp little "binks." "I made those up for you," he confessed shyly. "I made up whole songs and poems."

Grandmother covered herself quickly. "My mem-ory seems to be getting worse with every year."

"It's my fault," Wolf said sheepishly. "I never told you most of them."

"Even after you were married?" I asked.

When they both stared at me, I realized that I had spoiled the mood, but I thought it was so sweet to make up poems and songs for someone. Wolf stood there with the anxious expression of a man trying to re-gain his balance on a tightrope—as if he knew quite well we were not his family but was desperate to cling to the fantasy.

Fortunately, Grandmother made a shrewd guess. "But you were shy, weren't you?"

Wolf nodded in relief and said to me, "I couldn't even tell my parents what was the matter. They knew I was love-struck, but they didn't know who the girl was.

It drove them crazy. Fortunately, your mother wasn't so shy. She spoke to her parents, and they sent around the matchmaker."

"So it was an arranged marriage?" I asked.

"Some are more arranged than others." Grandmother laughed and glanced at Wolf. I think she was enjoying her role. Certainly, Wolf's story seemed romantic enough.

"Just so," he agreed. "Afterward, well, the family always seemed to be around."

"It's a shame in a way," Grandmother said, as if she felt sorry for that other woman, Wolf's real wife.

"You think so?" Wolf asked.

"I know so," Grandmother insisted.

Wolf and Grandmother chatted on. All he'd really wanted was an excuse to talk about his family.

And I felt as if Grandmother had opened a window just a crack so I could see into her world. I suppose if I was seven thousand miles away from China, I might like to talk with someone who shared the same kind of past.

It's a funny thing about a fantasy. When three people share it, it doesn't seem as crazy. And it doesn't seem nearly as fragile.

All the time he talked with Grandmother, Wolf worked at his stove, methodically taking care of one order after another until most of his customers had been satisfied. It was all I could do to keep from drooling while he cooked.

When he was down to just a couple of orders, he jerked his head at us. "Now, what would you like to eat? You could use a little fattening up," he said playfully. "Is there a famine back home?"

In a way, I felt pleased that he had accepted me as his Chinese daughter, and yet I did not know how to explain that I had to watch my diet because I was a dancer.

Grandmother jumped in, though. "I keep telling her she should eat more. But she wants to stay thin."

"I'll fix that," he said, returning to his stove. "What would you like?"

"Just some steamed vegetables," I said.

"See what I'm up against?" Grandmother sighed, but she was enjoying herself.

He smiled even wider. "She's stubborn. Just like you."

I decided to take a chance. "I have to stay in shape to dance."

"So you want to be a dancer," he said and considered the matter gravely.

Grandmother drew herself up just like her best friend, Madame, who was my ballet teacher. "She *is* a dancer. Very graceful."

"Fancy that," Wolf said as if he didn't mind embellishing the fantasy now.

"I do all right," I said cautiously.

He held up a palm and wagged it back and forth as if he was briskly polishing a window. "You don't have to be modest."

"Actually, my teacher is very pleased," I said, which was kind of the truth. Sometimes telling lies is like taking a sip of some exotic juice. "In fact," I added, "she assigned me an important role, Red Riding Hood."

"Wonderful, wonderful," Wolf beamed. "So you're a star."

Actually, the role wasn't very big, but it was fun to pretend I was a prima ballerina. "You could say that," I said—which wasn't exactly a lie since he had said it, not me.

"You should see her dance," Grandmother said.

I dug in the bag I had been carrying when Grandmother and I got pulled into the restaurant. "I wear these," I said. It took me a moment to pull open the drawstrings so I could take out my toe shoes.

Wolf fingered one of the shoe's satin ribbons, letting its softness trail off his fingers. "What funny shoes. Put them on and show me your new role."

THREE

The Star

Though I'd had only one rehearsal, I figured I could wing enough of it. I looked around at the crowded kitchen. "Here?"

Grandmother urged me on. "Don't be shy. You're very good."

I studied the hard linoleum. It would probably be my last choice for a stage. I knew Dr. Brown, Leah's mother, would shake her head. I had gotten hammer toes from practicing on concrete in my garage. To prevent any more damage, I'd promised to wear toe shoes and dance only on proper surfaces, like the ballet school's resilient wooden floor or in the practice room Leah's father had built for her.

But I didn't want to remind Grandmother of my problem. She'd nearly stopped me from taking dancing lessons altogether. So instead I tried another excuse. "I don't have any music," I protested.

"Hum," Grandmother said.

Self-consciously, I changed my shoes as Wolf watched. He was most interested when I tied the ribbons.

The waiter had come back and was standing, curious, by Wolf. "What odd shoes," he said, scratching his head.

Wolf turned to him. "Those are my daughter's dancing shoes," he explained proudly.

The dishwasher joined them. "Some country, isn't it? Just when you think you've seen everything, they come up with something like that."

Wolf seemed scandalized when I shed my jacket and sweats. "Isn't her costume a little tight?" he whispered to Grandmother.

"These are her practice clothes," Grandmother said, taking my jacket and folding it. "She usually wears nice costumes."

Wolf glanced in the direction of the dining room and the customers, most of whom were men. "I should hope so."

I tried to forget that I was in a kitchen, warm from the stove, and smelling of cooking oil and many different dishes. Getting to my feet, I began to do my exercises, trying to warm up quickly.

"How is she able to twist her legs that way?" Wolf wondered aloud to Grandmother when I set my heels together and turned my toes out.

"That's why she practices." Grandmother had folded up my clothes and held them on her lap.

"But is this the dance?" the waiter wanted to know.

"Not yet," I said. "Do you know the story of Red Riding Hood?"

When Wolf and the waiter shook their heads, I told them briefly. "She shouldn't have talked to strangers," Wolf decided when I finished.

"But the Wolf talked to her first," the waiter pointed out.

They might still be debating the issue if I hadn't cleared my throat loudly. "Madame," I said in Chinese, "Gentlemen. Red Riding Hood. Please imagine a forest in the background." With a sweep of my arm I indicated the kitchen walls.

I hummed a few bars from Red Riding Hood's music to myself. Rising on point slowly, I began to drift through the forest. Unfortunately, I found that I didn't remember the dance as well as I thought after just one practice and without the help of Leah and our other friend, Amy. I started to throw in whatever steps I could think of.

Wolf applauded. "She seems to float," he said to the waiter.

"Like a cloud," the waiter agreed.

It was my first try before an audience, so I maybe hammed it up too much, and I had to shorten my steps in the narrow confines of the kitchen. It also threw me off to have to explain things at certain moments like, "Now Wolf sees her and hides."

I performed the steps for being lost in the woods and then said, "And now Wolf springs into sight."

At that this point, I think I should have been running away scared, but I decided to improvise, and danced over to Wolf.

The cook folded his arms, looking very tough if not wolf-like. Remembering what I had told him, Wolf pantomimed asking me where I was going.

I pantomimed back that I was going to my grandmother's.

Raising a hand craftily, he waved good-bye and pretended to tiptoe on the shortcut as I danced off on the long route. By now, I was inventing everything. As I began a series of *pas de chats*, I crashed into a wall and fell on my backside.

"Are you all right?" Wolf asked in a worried voice.

Grandmother, though, had more faith in my abilities than I deserved. "She meant to do that."

"Really?" Wolf sounded doubtful.

I'd had more than my share of spills in my years of ballet. But my teacher had instructed me, "If you fall, pick yourself up and go on. And then work and work hard to correct the mistake before the next show." So I bounced back to my feet. "I'm fine," I said, but at the next rehearsal I would definitely pay attention to Madame's dance instructions, and I would definitely not make up any steps.

If my teacher could have seen me at that moment, I knew that my dancing would have driven her to despair, but fortunately the men didn't know any better. "Wonderful, wonderful," the waiter murmured. He was probably humoring Wolf, but I didn't care. This was far more encouraging than any reactions I had gotten this morning.

I shrugged back into my jacket and sweats. "That's it." I paused in the act of zippering the jacket up.

A tear was streaking down Wolf's broad cheek as he smiled. "You make me so proud," he whispered huskily.

"Praise a child, spoil a child," the waiter chided him in Chinese.

"That's for back in China, not here," he said, using the back of his hand to wipe away the tear. "Your dancing is so beautiful that it makes me sad."

At first, I thought I had heard him wrong. "Why are you so sad?"

"Because . . . because . . ." he struggled to explain. "You know how you dream of someone or something precious? You can hold that beautiful something." He reached out his hand and grabbed something invisible. "You can love it. Then you feel happy."

"Sure," I said.

"But when you wake up, it's gone." He opened his fingers and stared in wonder at his empty palm. "That's why it's beautiful and sad at the same time."

I thought of how often he must have dreamed

of his family, only to find them gone in the morning. I wanted to comfort him, but suddenly I felt all choked up.

He repeated the motion of grasping and releasing. "Perhaps that's what true beauty is. Something so lovely you never want to lose it, but the moment you reach for it, it disappears."

"Like your dreams," Grandmother said.

He tapped his leg. "Just so," he said. He spread his arms. "You've inspired me. You danced for me. Now let me perform my art for you. What dishes can I make for you?"

Grandmother said, "We'd like our favorites." She was really getting into her role.

"But not too much for me," I reminded him.

"I'll make my specialties." Turning, he marched proudly to his stove, and the dishwasher scurried back to his post.

Then the waiter escorted us into the dining room. While we had been in the kitchen, more customers had come in, so the restaurant was almost full again.

"Good, very good," he grunted, pulling out a chair. "I haven't seen him that happy in years." When he had helped Grandmother sit down at a table, he began to put out plates, bowls, and chopsticks—all of them courtesy of the Shanghai Low. The bowls had dragons chasing one another on them. When everything was set, he slipped two wrinkled dollar bills onto the table.

I slid them back toward him. "That's not why we're here."

The waiter tilted his head back and studied me from beneath long lashes—as if my words had surprised and puzzled him. "He wouldn't want pity," he finally said and shoved them back.

I stared at the two dollars. "Whatever happened to his real family?"

The waiter pressed his lips into a tight, disapproving line—as if we were prying too much.

I draped my jacket over the back of a chair and sat down with my bag next to me. "Please, I'd like to know," I said and slyly explained, "I don't want to say the wrong thing."

The waiter seemed to weigh the pros and cons, and after a great struggle finally informed us, "They starved."

Then he turned his back on us abruptly and squeezed his way on tiptoe between the tables to take an order.

No wonder the cook was so depressed, and no wonder he had wanted to pretend. Grandmother and I were both silent, thinking our own thoughts, until the kitchen door finally swung open and the waiter came out. "Here is the first course," he announced.

The restaurant fell silent as he made his way over to our table. As the waiter passed him, a man stood up. "Hey, that's not on the menu."

"Ah Wing, you wouldn't know artistry if it ran over you," the waiter said as he set a big, shallow bowl on our table.

In the center of the bowl was a basket formed by dense lattices of fried noodles. And in the bowl, swimming in broth, were vegetables and shrimps and quite a few things I didn't recognize.

"The Happy Family," he declared, and added for my sake, "the basket is made up of edible noodles." With his other hand he set down a big bowl of rice. "Just let the juices soften them up first."

I thought the name was ironic considering we were pretending that we were a family ourselves.

Grandmother's eyes admired the basket and then she sniffed the wonderful aromas rising from the Happy Family. "It smells delicious."

"Wolf will be pleased," the waiter said.

After many meals with Grandmother, I knew better than to ask what I was eating. I assumed "Happy Family" referred to the shrimps and other creatures in the bowl. Somehow, being cooked wouldn't be my idea of happiness, but I did have to admit that the soup tasted delicious.

When I was almost finished, I set my chopsticks over the bowl and shoved it away.

Like twin hawks, Grandmother's chopsticks hovered over the Family. "There's more than enough for me. Go ahead and eat."

"I can't," I said, staring at the bowl regretfully. The thought of what Madame would say kept my jaws clamped shut. And Leah and I had promised each other we'd keep our meals small because we both gained weight easily.

Grandmother shook her head. "You already look like you were made out of sticks. You're so scrawny people will think you come from a poor family that can't afford to feed you."

I tugged at a strand of hair. "So if I'm a blimp, it means we're rich?"

Grandmother took paper napkins from the dispenser and slid one over to me. "Now you know why I'd rather talk to Wolf. He takes me seriously."

Instantly, I regretted my smart mouth. "I'm sorry."

Grandmother sat back. "It's more your cousins, Georgie's and Eddy's children." She rolled her eyes heavenward. "Sometimes I think they're possessed."

My cousins were pretty bratty. "Sometimes I think the same thing."

Suddenly, the kitchen door flew open to reveal Wolf. He must have been peeking at us through the door's small diamond-shaped window. "What's wrong?"

"Nothing, nothing," Grandmother said.

In some distress, Wolf made his way toward us, followed closely by the waiter, "It used to be one of your favorite dishes."

"There's more?" I asked, stunned.

"Six courses in all," the waiter said, putting the platters down. He looked as if he was ready to snatch back his two dollars.

Wolf frowned at the Happy Family as if it had let him down. "I know you'll love the next dish." He started to turn back toward the kitchen.

"No, wait," I called to him in alarm. "I really can't eat any more."

Puzzled, he faced me again. "But you've barely tasted this one."

Hastily, I tried to apologize. "It's not your cooking. It's wonderful."

Grandmother set her chopsticks down. "She's supposed to be thin when she dances."

"Who wants to see scrawny dancers?" Wolf demanded. "Everyone will think they're skinny because they're so bad no one will pay them."

"Maybe it's easier to go on tiptoe when you're lighter," the waiter suggested.

As the rest of the restaurant began to debate the subject, Wolf spread his hands in frustration. "You're already much too thin." He glanced at Grandmother as if it were all her fault.

"So I've often told her," Grandmother defended herself. "But children nowadays won't listen."

"Won't you have a little more—just for me?" he coaxed.

I realized I was risking breaking the fantasy, but I wasn't about to blimp up before the coming recital. "I wish I could," I said.

"You listen to your father," the waiter scolded me. "He made this special for you."

Determined, Wolf picked up my chopsticks and clicked the tips over the Happy Family. "Come now. Just one little biteful." Selecting a shrimp, he raised the chopsticks toward me. "Open your mouth." He began to whistle like a bird. "Open your mouth, baby bird."

He was playing a game as if I were a three-year-old. I felt embarrassed as much for him as for me, but even so I resolved to resist. "Please don't ask any more." For a moment, we all held our breath, realizing that I might have gone too far.

Suddenly, Wolf lowered the chopsticks. "What am I doing? You're not a baby anymore. You're almost a young woman."

"Children grow up so quickly," Grandmother chimed in.

Each of us seemed to relax, as if we had managed to get the whole fantasy spinning again.

"Actually, I . . . I'm fasting," I improvised and anxiously watched how he would take that little fib.

He exhaled in relief. "Oh, it's religious."

I brightened. "Maybe I could take this home. Then, when the fast is done, I can finish it." I was sure it wouldn't go to waste with Dad in the house.

"You promise to eat it?" Wolf asked coyly.

"Who could turn down something as good as this?" I asked rhetorically.

"Only an idiot would," the waiter snapped.

"The food was wonderful," Grandmother said enthusiastically.

Wolf rocked up and down on the balls of his feet. "So I haven't lost my touch?" he asked, pleased.

"Not a bit," she assured him.

I glanced at the clock on the wall. On its face was an ad for a Chinese beer, and moving parts inside made it change from yellow to green to blue. It was already getting close to dinnertime. Mom would be worried.

I dabbed my mouth with a paper napkin. "You'll have to excuse me, but we have to leave now. I don't think there'll be time for the other courses."

He looked down ruefully at my almost clean bowl. "I hope you ate your vegetables at least."

"I'll see that she eats right," Grandmother reassured him.

Timidly, he extended a hand until it rested on my shoulder. "I don't want you to waste away," he said, patting me clumsily. He looked so sad. It almost broke my heart when I remembered how his real daughter had died. "Will you still be fasting next week?"

Next week? I guess we'd made the fantasy so comfortable for Wolf that he didn't want to let go now. I thought about dance lessons and schoolwork and my chores. Where would I find the time? I thought our good deed had been only for today. This was a lot more than I had bargained for. Helplessly, I glanced at the waiter, hoping he would rescue us. But he did his best to ignore the situation he had created.

I stalled, hoping that Grandmother would speak for us, but she remained silent, perhaps finding the situation as uncomfortable as I did. The pause had lasted a little longer than was polite, and Wolf's eyes began to flick desperately back and forth between us.

Finally I said, "Don't go to any trouble."

Wolf's shoulders sagged in relief. "You make it worthwhile," he said. He lingered, staring at me for a moment longer, and then returned to the kitchen.

I'd felt good while we had been playing the game, but now that it was over, I felt awful.

FOUR

The Race

The waiter started to pick up the platters of food. "I'll box everything for you."

I didn't think I wanted to try to explain to my folks how I had gotten an entire banquet. "You take it," I said to Grandmother. She lived in a little studio apartment next to Uncle Eddy's garage.

As he headed for the kitchen, the waiter jerked his head at the man who had commented on the menu. "Ah Wing, take them home."

He was in the middle of eating a rice plate heaped with spare ribs in pungent black bean sauce. "I'm on my break."

Though he was already balancing several platters, the waiter managed to whisk Ah Wing's plate from the table. "Not any more. You have a duty to the public—like a policeman or a fireman."

Ah Wing accepted the loss with good humor. From the back of his chair, he took a battered yellow cap with a cracked black leather visor. "Oh, yes, everyone looks up to cab drivers just like they do firemen." As the waiter went inside the kitchen, Ah Wing turned to Grandmother. "You wait here, lady. I'm parked down at the cab stand by the square. I'll swing around and pick you up."

As I told you, Grandmother could be very sensitive about her feet—especially if there was a crowd. "I can walk," she snapped. "I walked across China with a baby on my back and two small children."

"Feisty, aren't you?" Ah Wing said approvingly. "But I bet you didn't have these then." He tapped Grandmother's canes.

Those were fighting words to Grandmother. She jutted out her chin. "I'll race you."

Ah Wing, though, was already heading for the door. Laughing good-naturedly, he dismissed her efforts with a wave. "Some other day, when I've got more time."

Grandmother's eyes sparked as she heaved herself up on her canes. "Get up," she said to me.

I didn't want her hurting herself in her rush. "But you can't win the race," I protested from my chair.

"No, but I can start," she said. I could see how she had made it across China.

The waiter came out of the kitchen carrying a pink plastic bag filled with boxes. As soon as he saw Grandmother on her feet, he bustled over. "Wait till Ah Wing honks his horn."

She looked around the restaurant as if she wanted

everyone to hear. "I am not a cripple," she announced in a loud, clear voice.

"No one says you are." The waiter motioned to her empty seat. "So why don't you sit down?"

Grandmother thrust out an arm, which was a signal for me to help her into her coat. "Come, Robin."

"You are like his old woman," the waiter said, shaking his head.

As I guided Grandmother's arms into her coat sleeves, I asked, "You met her?"

"We went back to China together once. He told me all about her," he said and made his way to the front door.

Grandmother nodded as she buttoned her coat. "Pick up your bag, Robin," she said irritably. "Ah Wing's got a head start."

"Okay, okay." I followed Grandmother toward the door.

As we stepped out onto the street, the waiter handed me the bag of food. He pointed northward. "Go to Washington Street. Ah Wing will be heading up that way from the square."

Grandmother plunged into the tourists without another word. I could tell she was furious by the way her canes clicked on the sidewalk. "Thank you," I yelled back to the waiter and hurried after her.

"The idea," Grandmother snorted.

"They were just trying to make it easy for you," I said as I followed her.

She glanced over her shoulder. When she saw that the waiter had gone back inside, she eased up. "He's the one who should be taking it easy. He looks more beat up than my boots."

Now that I was alone with Grandmother, I wanted to ask her all the questions that had come to my mind in the restaurant. "Why didn't he bring his family over here?" I asked.

Grandmother dodged a tourist who had stopped suddenly to take a picture of a toothpick holder shaped like a toilet. "How much do you know about history?" By history I knew she meant Chinese-American history. I had to confess that I knew very little, except for the few things Grandmother had told me since she had arrived here recently from Hong Kong.

"American laws made it almost impossible for a man to bring his wife and children over," she explained. "So the men sent money home to their families. And every few years, if they were successful here, they would go home for a visit. That was the pattern."

The truth dawned on me slowly. "So for most of their lives, Wolf and his wife were like the man and woman in the song."

"Precisely." Grandmother leaned forward as a large person made his way past her. There were certain words that suited her British-Hong Kong accent beautifully and that was one of them.

"But if Wolf sent money home to them, how could they starve to death?" I asked.

"China's gone through a lot of political trouble in the last fifty years or more. And both before and after that period, there were famines in China. His family could have died at almost any time." Grandmother licked her lips as she considered where to start. "Lots of sorrows. For years, there was civil war between the Communists and Chiang Kai-shek's government. And then the Japanese came. And when we beat them, the Communists kicked Chiang Kai-shek out. That's when I left for Hong Kong with my family."

We were both silent for a moment, feeling sorry for the cook. Wolf could have lost his family at almost any time in the last fifty-nine years. That was a long time to be alone—even before Mom and Dad were born. It made me sad just thinking about it. And Wolf's song seemed even more poignant than before. I hated the thought that his song didn't have a happy ending, and it made me glad that we had given him a happy moment.

When we reached the corner, Grandmother turned right. "I want to show you something." She nodded toward Washington, which was jammed with traffic. "It's going to take Ah Wing a while to get through that."

We went about halfway down the block to a large square. At the west end were benches and concrete tables, and I saw a sign that said "Portsmouth Square." Sitting on the benches and playing games on the tables were many elderly Chinese men. There were at least two hundred of them. "They're all like the men in the song," Grandmother said. "They're all like Wolf in a way. Some of them came over as boys. They went back to China to get married and father children, but they always had to come back here to work."

I had had no idea of the scope. So many sad stories. So many sad lives.

"That's not fair," I said indignantly.

"Life rarely is fair," Grandmother muttered. She was busy watching the street. "Yoicks," she said. "Yoicks!" She raised a cane and wagged the tip in the air.

A pink-and-green cab chugged to a stop. It might have been spiffy back in the sixties, but it was so scraped and dinged that it looked ready for the scrap heap.

Amazed, Ah Wing poked his head out of the driver's window. "I told you I'd pick you up in front."

Grandmother surveyed the old car distastefully. "We didn't want to wait that long." She was already making her way to the curb.

"Well, I can't say I'm sorry." Ah Wing hopped out. "It would have taken a whole bunch of left turns to work my way over to the restaurant."

A long line of cars got held up behind his cab. As he helped us inside onto the worn vinyl seats, they began to honk. He didn't even seem to notice. I began to think that nothing bothered him. As he got back behind the wheel, he asked, "Where to?"

I wanted to go home, but suddenly I realized how late it must be. "I should have picked Ian up from the store by now," I said. It was too bad you couldn't do a good deed without getting in trouble.

"I'll talk to them," Grandmother said, and she gave Ah Wing the address.

"So you're out in the Richmond, are you?" he asked. The Richmond District was up in the northwest corner of San Francisco, by the ocean.

I noticed that the meter wasn't running. "Shouldn't you put your flag down?"

Ah Wing kept one hand on the wheel as he gestured with the other toward the silent meter. "Naw. I was just happy to finally get my order. Don't tell them at the Forest, or they'll raise their prices. But it's the best food in Chinatown. Wolf knows his way around a kitchen. If you can, come next weekend. Just give me a call. The ride will be free, too." He pulled down a sun visor, where a bunch of cards hung beneath a thick rubber band. It looked like it was holding the visor together as well.

Grandmother took the dirty, worn card and then exchanged a look with me. "I'm not sure." I thought she was just trying to be polite.

"We've both got a lot of stuff to do," I said to her, but it was really meant for Ah Wing. After all, this good deed was already going to get me into trouble.

"You Richmond Chinese," Ah Wing laughed.

"What's the matter? Chinatown not good enough for you?"

"We're just . . ." Grandmother hesitated. "Well, we're just busy."

"Aw, come on. Didn't you have fun today?" Ah Wing coaxed.

"None of your business," Grandmother snapped.

Ah Wing tried to draw Grandmother back into a conversation, but after that she would give him only curt, one-syllable answers. Ah Wing finally got bored and buzzed his dispatcher.

Ah Wing spoke a different dialect than we did so I didn't understand everything he said. I recognized a lot of numbers, though.

When I looked quizzically at Grandmother, she whispered in my ear. "He and the dispatcher are figuring out the numbers for their lottery tickets."

I settled back in the seat. "I can't wait till I tell my friends about our adventure."

Grandmother twisted around in horror. "No," she whispered, "you mustn't tell anyone."

"But we didn't do anything to be ashamed of," I argued. "In fact, we did a good deed."

Grandmother gave a deep sigh. "I should know better than to discuss things with you. You're a regular lawyer when it comes to twisting words."

I could be as hard-headed as she was. "I'm just trying to understand why I can't tell anyone."

She fiddled with the handles of her canes. "There are some things that are better left secrets."

I thought of her reaction to Wolf's song. "Like the butterfly earrings?"

Grandmother blushed. "Don't ever bring that up again with anybody—especially me."

"Why not?" I teased. "You never talk about when you were young in China."

I'd said the wrong thing. Grandmother's face became a stone mask. "Because some things are meant to be kept deep inside only."

"Deep inside, like here?" I touched my heart.

Grandmother nodded. "Especially that kind of secret." Then she looked away from me out the car window.

When she got that stony expression on her face, I knew better than to pry any more. Grandmother could shut up tighter than a clam when she wanted to. I'd only found out about her crippled feet by accidently barging in on her when she was undressing.

While Grandmother imitated the Great Wall, I listened to Ah Wing. The lottery was obviously a serious matter to him. As soon as he finished with his dispatcher, he asked Grandmother for her lucky numbers. "No one won the jackpot last week. It's up to thirty-one million dollars this week. If one of your numbers wins, I'll give you a share."

From the backseat, Grandmother huffed, "If I had any lucky numbers, I'd bet them myself."

"You could," he admitted generously and nodded toward a convenience store that had big banners on the window advertising that it sold lottery tickets. "Want me to pull over?"

Grandmother frowned disapprovingly. "I don't throw my money away."

Ah Wing twisted his rearview mirror so he could study Grandmother. "Are you sure you're Chinese?" he teased.

"I hold on to my money, if that's what you mean," Grandmother said.

Ah Wing rubbed his chin. "Chinese are cheap *and* Chinese gamble. Where do you think those two stereotypes come from?"

It was hard to dislike Ah Wing for long, and I guess Grandmother was amused because she surprised me by telling him the date of her birth. Hastily, he pulled a pen from the rubber band–bound sun visor and scribbled the number on a scrap of paper. Then he asked her for her children's birthdays. By the time they began working through her grandchildren, we were whizzing up Geary Boulevard. Traffic was so thick it took him a while to make a left turn, but then he was roaring past the stores and restaurants.

In the twilight, lines were beginning to appear in front of the good restaurants. And there were the usual bad restaurants, where worried waiters hovered in the doorway, trying to entice someone inside. Dad used to say that you could begin at one end of Geary and eat your way to the ocean and then start over with the new restaurants that had opened up.

Finally I saw Mad George's bazaar. The blue-tiled facade framed big picture windows through which I could see piles of electronic merchandise. Parked in front of the store was a huge blue truck with a crane, and dangling by ropes was a huge yellow sign with black lettering.

Beneath the sign stood Mom and her two brothers, engaged in their usual occupation: arguing. Uncle George was supposed to put up his expertise, Uncle Eddy the money, and they were both trying to talk Mom into giving up her accountant's job to manage the store. But they hadn't been able to agree on anything else.

Uncle Georgie had dreams of expanding his stores until he could rival the big chains of electronic discounters. And he'd talked Uncle Eddy and Mom into helping him. Uncle Eddy had taken out a second mortgage on his house to provide additional capital, and Mom went right to the store after finishing her regular day job. By the time she got home, she was so tired and frustrated, she wound up quarreling with Dad, too.

Grandmother sighed as Ah Wing pulled up to the curb beyond the crane. "They were bickering when we left, and they're still at it."

"Maybe it was nicer being Wolf's family," I tried to joke.

"Maybe it was," Grandmother agreed.

Ah Wing checked for a space in traffic, then sprang out and ran around to open the curbside passenger door.

"All ashore, who's going ashore?" Ah Wing said cheerfully.

"You sure we can't pay you?" Grandmother asked.

"You just did, lady. Make Wolf happy, and you make me happy." He slapped his stomach for emphasis.

Impulsively, Grandmother opened her purse. "Here," she said. I recognized the two frayed dollar bills. "Play them for me."

Ah Wing's face lit up. "So you are Chinese, after all. How will I call you if you win?" he asked as he took the money.

"I'll give you my phone number," Grandmother said.

Taking off his battered old cap, he slipped another card from under the visor and handed it to Grandmother. "Write it on this."

As if they were concluding a multimillion-dollar deal—I guess in their own minds they were—he solemnly handed her the pen and the card.

When Grandmother returned the card and pen to him, Ah Wing touched the cap's visor. "We're partners now, so don't be a stranger. Call me next week. I'll give you a free ride to Chinatown."

Grandmother bit her lip. "I can't."

Ah Wing sounded sad. "He'll be disappointed."

"It can't be helped." Her eyes happened to fall on the bag of food, which still rested, open, between my feet. Heavenly aromas were coming from it. "Here. You need this more than we do." Picking up the bag, she slid it onto the front seat.

Ah Wing beamed. "You're all right, lady."

I slid across the seat after Grandmother and stepped onto the sidewalk. "Thanks."

"Anytime." As he took off, we waved.

"I feel like Cinderella after midnight, and there goes our carriage," I said. I was no longer the star ballerina but merely a student.

Grandmother leaned forward to study me. "You were altogether too good at making up stories, young lady."

I defended myself quickly. "Madame says I have a vivid imagination. That's why I'm good at improvisations."

When I invoked the name of her special friend and mentor in American life, Grandmother raised her eyebrows slightly. "I don't think Madame had this in mind."

I zipped my jacket all the way up to the collar as we walked toward the store. "It was warmer in Chinatown."

Grandmother fussed over me by pulling the zipper up the last millimeter. "The Chinese always know where to live," she insisted.

When Grandmother made pronouncements like that, I usually humored her. This time, however, I really did agree. In the growing cold and gloom, it was hard to cling to any more dreams.

"You're a jerk, Georgie," we heard Uncle Eddy suddenly shout.

FIVE

Mad George

Mom and my uncles were so caught up in their argument that they didn't even notice Grandmother and me approach them.

"The sign is loud. It is ugly, and it is crude," Mom complained to Uncle Georgie.

"You don't often find a sign that can combine all three." Uncle Georgie gazed up at the sign almost with affection. "Got to attract people's attention. We're playing with the big boys now, but we don't have their budget for advertising. So we got to get them in here any way we can. Because once they try Mad George's, good customer relations and quality products will keep them coming back."

"So in the meantime we outdo our rivals in taste-lessness?" Eddy asked.

"Who cares about taste so long as they remember?" Uncle Georgie smacked his lips. "Wait till you see the

TV spots I got planned." He glanced at Mom. "By the way, have you spoken to Gil about shooting them?"

Mom stared up at the sign. "Gil would never do it. He'd rather be dropped in boiling oil than work on any commercial. Artistic integrity and all that."

"Work on him," Uncle Georgie urged. "Use a little honey." He wriggled his hips in illustration.

Mom folded her arms. "You're disgusting."

"Just like his sign." Uncle Eddy waved his hand over his head toward the monstrosity.

Uncle Georgie jerked a thumb toward his chest. "You don't know the business like I do. You can't bring customers in if they don't notice you."

Uncle Eddy ran a hand through his thinning hair. One of these days he was going to do that once too often and find there was nothing there. "Fine, why don't you hire elephants and brass bands, too?"

Uncle Georgie's lip curled in a sneer. "Because you have to hire clean-up crews, too, if you get elephants. You don't think, Eddy. That's why the competition's always one step ahead of you."

Grandmother sighed as if her pleasant fantasy in Chinatown was now quite far away. Throwing back her shoulders resolutely, she stumped among them, thumping one of her canes upon the pavement. "Enough."

She didn't speak very loudly, and the traffic on Geary drowned out the sound of her cane, but her grown-up children instantly became silent.

"Mama," Mother said, looking embarrassed, "how long have you been here?"

"Long enough," Grandmother snorted, eyeing each of her children. As she stared at them, one by one they dropped their heads.

"Was the landlord in?" Uncle Eddy asked.

"Yes. I paid the store's rent and here's the receipt." Grandmother dug out a slip of paper and handed it to Mom, who was keeping the books.

"You were gone a lot longer than we thought," Mom said.

"I . . . uh . . . met an old friend," Grandmother ad-libbed.

It was my turn to stare at Grandmother. Well, I guess you could call Wolf a friend. But from her dead-pan expression, you never would have known she was twisting the truth. I could see where I had gotten my talent for improvisation.

"You could have called," Mom scolded me, not Grandmother—even though I wasn't the boss.

"Now don't blame Robin," Grandmother said. She changed the subject by tilting her head back to look up at the sign.

Uncle Georgie proudly waved a hand at it. "What do you think? It'd stand out in Hong Kong, and Hong Kong has a lot of signs."

"That's just the trouble," Uncle Eddy growled.

She continued to gaze up at it. "Did you pay for it?"

"Yes," Uncle Georgie said, as if that was the cleverest thing.

"Well," Grandmother sighed and turned to Uncle Eddy, "you needed a sign."

"But we voted for a different sign, Mother," Uncle Eddy protested.

"Next time, go with Georgie and make sure he follows the vote," Grandmother said.

Mom turned to Uncle Eddy. "You better go with Georgie when he orders the business cards."

"Too late," Uncle Georgie declared triumphantly. "I ordered them already. I got them in neon red." He turned to the crane operator and motioned for him to go ahead.

Uncle Eddy balled his hands into fists. "But Elaine and I didn't get to help pick them out. It's not fair." At that moment, he sounded just like a five-year-old boy.

"You snooze; you lose," Uncle Georgie taunted with a snap of his fingers.

"Georgie, Eddy, can't we get along?" Mom begged.

Uncle Eddy puffed out his chest. "Not with this jerk."

"I said that's enough," Grandmother snapped.

"But Mother," Uncle Eddy whined.

"The money's spent. It's too late," Grandmother said to him firmly.

"Yes, Mother," Uncle Eddy grunted.

As Uncle Georgie began to grin in triumph, it was

his turn in the hot seat. "And before you make a major decision next time, you ask me first, Georgie."

"Yes, Mother," Uncle Georgie said meekly.

When Grandmother was with her children, she could keep them from quarreling. Her job was to play referee and peacemaker. She smiled at me resignedly as if we all had sacrifices to make for the family.

With the cease-fire in effect, Mom could think of other things. She glanced at her watch and then looked at me reproachfully. "Ian's been working here too long. He should have gone home an hour ago to have dinner."

Ever since the store opened Mom had been plain cranky. I tried to tell myself that it was probably from lack of sleep because she was holding down her regular job too, but that didn't make the scolding any easier.

I wished I could have told Mom about our good deed, but in the mood she was in, she'd probably just blow her stack. I remembered what Grandmother had said in the taxicab about keeping a secret. Maybe this was what she had been trying to tell me. There had been something special about our afternoon with Wolf. For a few brief hours, Grandmother had been able to go back to her youth in China. It had been nice to be with someone who cared. So you wanted to protect it inside you—especially from our quarreling family.

I felt my shoulders tensing, ready for a tongue-lashing, but Grandmother sprang to my defense. "Now don't go blaming Robin. It was all my fault."

Mom's face was a real study. She was still suspicious, but she could hardly call her own mother a liar.
Grandmother took over the situation by turning toward the sign.

"You certainly can't miss the sign," she said.

Like the dutiful daughter she was, Mom pivoted.
"That's the one thing you can say for it."

"Why don't you go get your little brother and take
him home," Grandmother hinted. She was offering me
an escape.

Reality closed in like a cage. I could expect dreary
hours of watching Wolf Warrior cartoons with my
brother now. "Don't you want to visit us, Grandmother?" I asked her eagerly.

Maybe a little too eagerly in Mom's judgment.
"Grandmother's tired. She should go home."

"No, I think I'll stay here and help a little," she said.
She arched her eyebrows as if to ask: How else can I
keep my children from killing one another?

As I stepped inside Mad George's, I looked at the
pyramids of camcorders in their boxes, and the walls of
televisions all tuned to MTV's latest find. The music
collided with the rap music coming from the wall of
stereos opposite. I didn't see how anyone could think
in this din.

Uncle Georgie's oldest son, Henry, had to shout to
make himself heard. "No, sir. You have to bring in either an ad or a signed note with their price on it."

The customer, a boy in a long blue raincoat and

baggy trousers, pointed at the sign. "You just say you'll beat any price. And the sales guy at Circuit City told me theirs was only fifty-nine bucks."

Henry rolled his eyes. "You need written proof, sir."

"Are you calling me a liar?" The customer slapped his chest angrily.

I scooted past them. So much for good customer relations.

At a nearby counter, a half-dozen small boys were playing Nintendo on a demonstrator. Except for them and Henry's customer, there was no one else taking advantage of my crazy uncle. And he wanted to add more stores.

Suddenly, one of the black-haired heads swiveled away from the game screen. "Oh, it's you," Ian frowned. "You're late."

The best defense was a good offense. "You're not supposed to play those violent games yet," I scolded him. Ian was only seven.

"But I'm winning," he said.

"Don't let Mom catch you," I warned, nodding outside. "She thinks you're working."

"I am. I'm demonstrating," Ian said. "Anyway, she's too busy to notice me now." Ian was trying hard to be tough, but I could see his lip quivering. He was as unhappy about the changes in our lives as I was.

"Things'll be okay," I whispered, ruffling his hair. "Remember? We talked about that. Once Uncle

Georgie's store does better, we'll get our old mom back."

Ian glanced quickly at his friends, but they were still engrossed in the maneuvers of a little blue creature wearing a miner's cap. "Not in front of the guys," he complained, trying to slap his hair back into place.

I grinned. "Sorry, Macho Man."

Lately Ian lost his temper if you so much as looked at him the wrong way. He scowled up at me. "All I know is that they didn't start arguing until you made such a big deal about that stupid ballet." Whirling around, he tried to rejoin his friends at the game.

He'd struck a sore spot on my conscience. When we were originally trying to bring Grandmother over from Hong Kong, Mom had wanted to save money by stopping my lessons. Dad had sided with me about their importance and that had caused friction with Mom. To Mom, Dad and I had been selfish and had not thought of the entire family. Even though Grandmother had solved the problem and I was back at ballet, Mom and Dad had taken the fight on to new arenas. Uncle Georgie's business was the reason for the latest championship bout.

I caught him. "It's not just my fault, you know."

Seeing the hostile expression on his face, I couldn't remember the last time the four of us had all been happy together. Suddenly I felt very tired. "Come on. I'm taking you home."

Ian tried to twist free. "I'd rather stay here."

Ordering him to come would only make Ian dig in his heels. So instead, I warned, "If you stay, you change the schedule. And you know how our parents have been lately. Any change in the schedule makes them mad. You don't want them getting mad, do you?"

He stopped wriggling. "No."

"Then let's go." When I released him, he almost fell backward but caught himself.

"I was winning," he said.

As I headed outside, I couldn't help muttering, "I'm glad someone in the family is."

SIX

Home, Sweet Home

Ian said nothing on the way home, and I kept thinking about Wolf. What a sad life. I told myself that Grandmother and I had done a good deed. With a guilty twinge, I thought maybe I could tell Dad. Any man who would spend three months in a rain forest filming parrots had to have more of a sense of adventure than Mom.

Our set of flats has the same layout as hundreds in the Richmond District. It crowded right up to the sidewalk so there was no front yard. In fact, there wasn't a tree on the block. On the ground floor was the garage we shared with the Aguilars. The Aguilars' flat was on the next floor, and ours was on the top floor. A staircase led up from the street to the second floor, where there were two doors, one leading into the Aguilars' flat and the other to the stairs for ours.

Mrs. Aguilar must have been to the laundromat because she was walking down the sidewalk pushing a metal cart full of neatly folded clothing. "Evening, Mrs. Aguilar," I said, catching up with her.

Mrs. Aguilar was a short, pleasant woman. "Good evening, Robin. How is the dancing?"

They could hear me practicing my ballet steps above their heads. "Fine," I said.

At almost the same time, Ian scowled, "Lousy."

I made a point of ignoring the little creep. "Have I been bothering you?"

Mrs. Aguilar hesitated. "Well, we do hear a radio at night sometimes."

Their bedroom was right below Ian's. "Ian won't do that again."

Mrs. Aguilar smiled in relief. "Thank you. By the way, I saw your new store. Your family is so industrious."

Mrs. Aguilar didn't know the half of it. I just wanted to get home now, but I knew what Mom would have wanted us to do. "Can we help you up the steps?"

"Well, I wouldn't mind. It's such a very long set of steps." With Ian and me lifting from below and Mrs. Aguilar pulling from above, we got her laundry up the stairs to her front door. When she opened her door, the most wonderful spicy smells came out of her flat. My stomach began to growl.

Ian must have felt hungry, too. When we left her, he said, "I'm starved."

"Dad will have something ready for us," I said, fishing my keys from my bag.

"It will probably be burnt," Ian scowled.

As I trudged up the staircase, I noticed how dirty the steps were. I remembered that I was supposed to clean our place that week but there never seemed enough time between school, chores, and ballet.

Our own flat smelled dusty when I opened the door, but there were no odors of cooking or burning food—which was funny.

"Dad?" I called, but there wasn't any answer. And when I went into the kitchen, there wasn't anything on the stove.

"Where's dinner?" Ian asked in disgust.

"Maybe there's something in the fridge," I said. But when I looked in the refrigerator, all I found were some dried-out apples.

"I'm hungry," Ian whined.

With regret I thought of the banquet that we had given to Ah Wing. My stomach rumbled just at the thought of it.

"Want an apple?" I asked.

Ian began rooting around in the refrigerator himself. Frustrated, he looked up at the list on the refrigerator door. "Dad didn't even shop for food."

"He probably got caught up in his film project. You know how he is," I said. Though Dad had a job in a camera shop, he was really a documentary maker. As he said, the trick wasn't shooting the film, it was getting the funds to make the picture.

At that moment, the culprit himself came into the kitchen. "I thought I heard voices," Dad said cheerfully.

The moment I saw his orange shirt and green pants, I knew Mom and he must have had a fight that morning. "What did you say to Mom this morning?"

Dad looked down at his tie. "What's wrong? Doesn't it match?"

My father was color-blind, so he depended on Mom to lay out his clothes before he went to work. "Nothing, but the tie is purple. Your shirt is orange and your pants are green," I said.

Ian didn't help any by pointing at Dad and laughing so hard that he fell to the linoleum floor.

"I guess in the middle of discussing things, your mom didn't notice." Dad's face turned beet red.

He and Mom had been "discussing" things a lot. Lately, Dad had been wearing a lot of loud outfits.

Not wanting him to brood about Mom's trick, I started to tell him about our adventure. "Dad. The craziest thing happened—"

Dad hooked his arm through mine. "Not now, Robin. You've got to help me. I got a call to meet with some people who may be willing to put up some money for my documentary. I've been working on my presentation all afternoon. But I guess I need your help getting dressed."

So that's why he hadn't cooked dinner, or even shopped for food. I squeezed Dad's arm. "Then we better get you dressed up."

We went down the hallway to his and Mom's bedroom, and I selected a blue shirt and gray slacks from the closet. "Something casual but not too casual," I said and got out a red tie. "And I read somewhere that this is the 'official power color of the week.'"

"I'll check with you in the morning," Dad said as I handed him the clothes.

"The funniest thing happened today—" I started again to tell him about Wolf and Grandmother.

He put his hand against my back and gently shoved me toward the door. "Can't talk now, honey. Got to scoot."

I couldn't help comparing my real father to Wolf. He'd wanted to know all about my dancing, and if he'd had his way, he would have stuffed me like a turkey.

He was already closing the door when I turned in the hallway. "Knock 'em dead, Dad," I said.

"The project should sell itself," Dad said excitedly as he shut the door in my face.

Ian was still in the kitchen. I saw that he was crying. "I want Grandmother. I want things the way they were."

Even if he blamed me for the fights at home, my shoulder was the only available one on which to cry. I sat there and held him while he did just that. He seemed like my little brother again—not the brat at the video store. "I know, I know," I said. "I want the same things."

Maybe Mad George would get in the black so my uncles could hire a bookkeeper and let Mom quit. Maybe Dad would find an angel to back his film. Then both Mom and Dad would be happy and stop fighting and we could get back to normal. It was a lot of "maybes," though.

As I held Ian, I couldn't help thinking about Wolf. It was such a shame that all that love inside him was going to waste. He had made me feel good as his daughter. In fact, it had been the nicest part of my day, next to ballet lessons.

At that moment, Dad popped in to say good-bye. When he saw the open refrigerator door, he slapped his forehead. "Oh, no, I was supposed to shop, wasn't I?"

Ian turned his tear-blurred face toward Dad. "Nobody has time for us," he said and began to cry all over again.

Dad looked as if Ian had just kicked him in the gut. "Ian, Robin, I'm so sorry."

I knew how important this meeting was to him.

"It's okay," I said. "Go to your meeting, Dad."

He hovered uncertainly. "But . . ."

"I can handle it," I said. I'd have to.

I heard Dad walking slowly down the stairs, like a man going to his execution, and a moment later the front door slammed shut.

While Ian got the tears out of him, I tried to re-member how much money I had from baby-sitting—it had been a while since I'd had the time to watch other people's children. Still, I thought I'd have enough. "You want a pizza?"

He perked up at that. "With double sausage?"

"It may have to be just a regular pizza," I said. I wiped his wet cheeks. "Okay?"

When he nodded, I helped him get up. Once I had him safely in front of the television and had popped in a Wolf Warriors tape, I went to my room and counted my change. It would be close.

I did my homework and Ian watched cartoons until the doorbell rang. I ran down the stairs. At the front door was a teenager in street clothes, but on his head was a paper cap with orange and red stripes. "Medium pizza?"

"Yeah." When I took the pizza, I noticed the bill taped on top of the box. Too late, I realized that I hadn't figured on tax. I counted out the dollar bills and coins, filling both his cupped palms.

"What'd you do? Break your piggy bank?" he sneered.

I had a quarter to spare when I was finished. Be-cause of that remark I hesitated to add it as a tip, but he had brought the pizza on time. "And something for your troubles," I said, flipping the quarter on top of the pile of change.

He stuffed everything into a pocket. "Thanks. Now I can get a Porsche," he smirked.

"Have fun driving," I said. Closing the door, I brought the pizza upstairs. Ian was already at the head of the stairs. "Oh, boy."

He kept right by my elbow all the way into the kitchen and began to eat even as I got out two plates. The little pig would have eaten more than half if I had let him. I'd taken only one slice. "Leave the rest for Mom. She's expecting dinner to be waiting. And you know how Dad is. He'll probably have forgotten to eat," I reminded him.

Reluctantly, he returned the piece to the box. I carefully put the pieces in plastic wrap and put them into our refrigerator.

Ian was still watching the cartoons and I was doing homework when Mom got home around nine-thirty. She dragged herself into the living room. "What a day I've had. Had to get all our vendors to give us extensions and then hound all the deadbeats."

I tried to make it up to her. "Then sit down and I'll nuke some pizza for you."

Mom frowned. "Didn't Dad make dinner?"

"Dad was busy," Ian said.

Mom got that stormy expression on her face, as if there were going to be more "discussions."

"He was supposed—" she began to say.

"It's not his fault. He got a call from a possible

backer," I said quickly in his defense. "He was busy preparing."

"Not that movie again." With a groan, Mom sank down into a chair. "I wish he'd never seen a camera."

And I bet he wished Mom had never joined Mad George's, I thought but had enough sense not to say. "We handled it, Mom. We left some in the fridge for you and Dad."

Mom rubbed her cheeks. "Lately we've had to leave a lot for you to handle, haven't we?"

I shrugged. "We understand."

Mom smiled like her old self. "I need a hug."

Ian went to her right away. She put her left arm around him and held out her right arm. "A double one."

I thought I was too old for hugs, but I guess I was wrong. It felt good. And for a moment, I could almost pretend that things were getting better.

SEVEN

The Master Chef

The next morning, I woke to the rumbling noise. I was so sleepy that at first I thought we might be having thunder and lightning, which is pretty rare in San Francisco. As consciousness slowly increased, I realized I was just hearing Mom and Dad's voices through the wall.

I rolled over, trying to shut out the angry sounds by covering my head with my pillow, but I couldn't breathe. Eventually I just gave up hiding and sat up. It was hard to remember how I used to love Sundays, when our whole family would enjoy different outings—the zoo, the houseboats in Sausalito, the view from Mount Tamalpais.

When they continued to shout, I closed my eyes and tried to remember what it was like to be a star—even if I was only dancing in a kitchen. And to be loved and protected. At that moment I wanted to be part of a fantasy family as much as Wolf did. And I found myself yearning to be back in Chinatown in his kitchen.

Nowadays, my parents turned anything into another battlefield. My adventure in Chinatown was too special to be treated that way. Grandmother had been right. There were some things better kept secret.

Sunday was Dad's normal gig at the camera store, and Mom and Ian left for Mad George's. I emerged from my room to find the Sunday paper scattered all over the flat. I went along the hallway and from room to room to gather it up.

After I read what I could, I checked the kitchen and found it freshly stocked. Our local supermarket operated a full twenty-four hours, so I guess Mom had gone out shopping early that morning before she headed over to Mad George's.

After my binge at the Celestial Forest, though, I confined myself to half a grapefruit for breakfast and then spent most of the day trying to practice what I remembered of Red Riding Hood's steps. I figured that after the catastrophe in Wolf's kitchen, I'd better concentrate on my dancing.

First, I went back to basics and practiced my fundamentals to make sure my technique hadn't gotten sloppy. I was still practicing in the living room in the late afternoon when the front door slammed. "Who's ready for a feast?" Dad shouted up the stairs.

"How did it go last night?" I asked, walking out into the hallway.

Dad stormed up the stairs with a grocery bag in either arm. Mom had dressed him in brown slacks with a purple shirt, so I knew their "discussion" this morning must have been a doozy. "They did a lot of smiling and clapping, but in the end they said they had a lot of other proposals to evaluate first."

I took one of the bags from him. "Isn't that what the other foundations said, too?"

Dad charged into the kitchen as if he wanted to forget the topic of our conversation. "Yep. No one wants to be the first to take a risk."

"Sorry," I said, trying to keep up with him.

"I've done my best, but those decisions aren't under my control. So," poor Dad forced himself to sound cheerful as he began to empty his bag's contents onto the table, "I thought I'd make up for yesterday's famine."

I felt a twinge of guilt for some of the things I had been thinking. "It'd be nice to eat as a family," I said over the clattering of bottles and cans.

While I took the things out of my bag, Dad rummaged around in the cabinets. "We haven't been able to do that much, have we?"

Dad usually wasn't this eager to cook. I thought he might be trying to work off some of his disappointment. I assumed he was searching for the pots and pans, so I went to one of the lower cabinets and opened the doors for him. "Things will get better when you get your movie off the ground and Mom makes Mad George's into a success."

"Wouldn't that be nice?" He peered deep into the shadows of the cabinet. "Do you know where the small pot is?"

"Right in front of you," I said and nudged him to the side. When he moved out of my way, I got the smaller pot from the top of a stack. "Maybe I'd better help you cook."

Dad nodded his thanks as he took it. "Now quit worrying. It was only a couple of accidents in the kitchen."

Dad could operate cameras in the jungle and underwater and from a crane and dangling by a rope down a cliff, and if I wanted someone to film me climbing Mount Everest, I would choose him. But he was hopeless in the kitchen. It was even odds that he knew which end of a kitchen knife to hold.

As I helped him tie his apron strings, I reminded him, "The fire department had to come for the last one. It's not like they give volume discounts to their customers."

Dad waved the pot over his head. "Well, all that is over. I'm sorry about all the shouting that's been going on between your mother and me. That's been happening too much lately. And I thought over what Ian said. So tonight I am going to cook for all of us. We're going to have a sit-down meal like a real family. I called your mom and invited her to dinner tonight."

I folded up the paper bags for recycling. "What's on the menu?"

Dad grabbed me by the shoulders and steered me toward the door. "Relax for a change. You're supposed to be a guest. It won't mean the same if I let you do everything." I was about to protest, but we heard the front door open. "That would be Mom or Ian. Go and be nice."

When I stepped outside, I saw Mom and Ian mounting the stairs to our apartment. "But I want to eat at Brian's house," Ian was protesting as Mom dragged him up the steps.

"You've been saying that you wanted to do things together. Well, this is it," Mom snapped. She held on to her briefcase with one hand and Ian with the other. "So what kind of takeout are we having tonight?"

I pirouetted and waved my hands at the kitchen door. "Tonight, you will have the personal services of that world-famous chef, Monsieur Gil."

Right on cue, Dad waltzed into the hallway. Ian instantly started to giggle at the sight of Dad in an apron.

"Welcome, welcome to our humble eating establishment," Dad said. Stripping off his oven mitts and tucking them under his arm, he helped Mom take her coat off. As I eased my brother out of his jacket, he whispered to me, horrified, "You're letting Dad cook?"

"You weren't so worried last night. And anyway, I couldn't stop him," I said.

Mom just stood in the hallway with her briefcase crammed with paperwork from the store. "What happened?"

Dad got louder and friendlier than usual, the more nervous he got. "Nothing happened," he said, kissing her and taking her briefcase. "I decided that we haven't been doing enough stuff together as a family, so I'm going to cook dinner tonight." He handed me Mom's briefcase.

"But I picked up some frozen dinners this morning," Mom protested.

"If we're not eating takeout, we're eating *cuisine arctique.* For once, you're going to have a home-cooked meal. Would you like something to drink?" Dad asked.

"Water would be nice." To simplify things for Dad, she added, "No ice."

Mom took her briefcase back from me as I escorted her down the hallway toward the living room. "This isn't one of your crazy notions, is it, Robin?" she accused me.

Lately, Mom had been so tense from working at the store that she was always ready to pick a fight. Most of the time it was with Dad. Some of the time, though, it was with me. I tried to become like Teflon. "The idea is one hundred percent, unadulterated Dad," I said, "but I don't see what's wrong with it."

"You'll know when the Fire Department comes," Mom mumbled pessimistically.

As Mom sat down on the sofa, Dad came in with two glasses of water. "Here you are, honey." Handing her one, he plopped down beside her and set his glass on an end table.

Mom instantly jumped to her feet, afraid Dad's glass would stain the wood. Lifting it, she slid a magazine on the table before she put it down again.

"Is that instinct or what?" Dad asked, teasing her.

Mom smiled sheepishly. "Sorry." But when she had taken her seat again, she put a magazine on the coffee table beneath her own glass, too. "How's your movie coming?" Mom asked. "I meant to ask you this morning."

"Great, great." Dad's head bobbed up and down in his eagerness. "I think I've got a group willing to donate ten thousand to the cause."

That wasn't what he had told me, but I guess he was trying to put the best spin on things.

"Wonderful," Mom said.

"How's Georgie's business?" Dad asked. He added shyly, "I meant to ask you this morning, too."

"It could not be better," Mom said. That was a direct contradiction of what I had seen and heard, but I kept my mouth shut.

At that moment, Mom and Dad reminded me of two people doing a stately dance. Holding hands, they kept circling and circling, unable to separate and unable to come closer together. It was agonizing to watch.

Then I smelled something funny in the air. "I'll get

more water," I said, using that as an excuse to go to the kitchen.

Too late. Mom could smell it, too. "Gil, is something burning?"

Dad snatched up his mitts and jumped to his feet. "No, no, everything's under control. The gravy's supposed to caramelize—like flan."

"Oh, really? So fancy," Mom said uncertainly.

"Well, I thought you'd like a change of pace." And he dashed into the kitchen. In a moment, we heard a lot of pots clanking and water rushing in the sink.

Mom's gaze followed Dad guiltily. He was still in the loud, mismatched clothes. "I wonder if he'd like some help?" I took that as a positive sign.

"I'll take care of it," I said, starting to rise. "You're our guest."

"That's all right. Don't embarrass him," Mom said. That showed more sensitivity for Dad's feelings than usual. Unfortunately, it meant Mom could aim all her artillery at me instead. "There isn't any chance you could give us more help in the store, is there?"

"Grandmother and Dad said I could take ballet," I said quickly.

"That's lessons, but do you really have to be part of this recital?" Mom asked. She was always trying to reduce my involvement in ballet. First, the excuse had been money problems, and now it was a question of time.

Mom didn't understand at all. "It's what the lessons

lead to," I said as I headed for the kitchen. "I'm thirsty. I think I'll get a glass of water for myself."

It was chaos in the kitchen. Dad had the window open and was using a dish towel to fan the smoke out. The pot was black in the sink. I ran water into it.

"I so wanted this meal to go well," Dad sighed.

"Don't give up just yet." I jerked open the pantry door to see what else Mom had bought that morning. "There're cans of pork and beans in the cabinet," I said and looked into the freezer. "And frozen hot dogs." And out of the fridge, I took a loaf of sourdough bread. "And this will be okay toasted. We've got the makings of Ian's favorite dinner."

Dad went on flapping the towel at the window, while I took a new pot from a cabinet. "What would I do without you, honey?"

I got the cans from the pantry. The can opener wasn't in its usual spot, so I had to dig around before I found it hanging from the same hook as the whisk. "You'd starve, of course." I handed the bread off to him like a football. "You're in charge of the toast." As long as I kept an eye on him, it would go okay.

As Dad stuck the first pieces into the toaster, he said, "At dinner, let's make sure we create a warm, nurturing atmosphere for your mother and brother." He quoted it stiffly as if he had memorized something from a magazine article.

I suppose that explained his loud, puppy-like behavior. "Okay, Dad." I hurried around the kitchen, dumping the contents of the cans into the pot and then adding the frozen hot dogs.

In no time, we had the pork and beans bubbling on the stove.

I set the table while I kept an eye on Dad and the dinner so that one or the other didn't burn. When everything was ready, I poured the main course into a soup tureen. "Take out the toast, Dad," I said, nodding to a plate piled with a stack of golden-brown toast.

I followed Dad at a careful distance to the table. When our dinner had safely arrived, I took the apron off Dad. "Now get Mom."

"But what do I say?" he asked, staring dubiously at a hot dog slanting up from a brown sea of beans.

I straightened his hair and then his collar. "Tell Mom that we were going to cook something fancier, but we thought we'd make Ian guest of honor tonight."

"But we burned a pot," Dad said.

"You were caramelizing the pork and beans." I took a step back and made a frame with my hands to study the view.

Dad suddenly smiled like the father I remembered. "I'd be lost without you."

"And don't you forget it," I said, giving him a quick kiss for good luck and a push toward the living room.

EIGHT

My Dinner with Mom

I could hear Dad turning on the charm as he made the dinner announcement to Mom. As he fussed over her, I went to get my little brother. The hallway seemed darker than usual as I knocked at his door.

"Dinner," I said.

"Did Dad really cook it?" he asked warily through the closed door.

"No, I did," I said. I didn't want him staying in his room through dinner. "Now come on out. You're guest of honor."

"What does that mean?" he asked as he opened his door and stepped out of his room. Then he caught a whiff of dinner. "Pork and beans!" And the next moment he was scampering down the hallway.

When I sat down at the table with my family, it almost seemed like the old days before Mom went to work for Uncle Georgie. If Mom was surprised by the menu, she hid it well.

"Oh, boy." Ian reached out with the serving spoon and stabbed it into the steaming bowl.

"Ian." Mom grabbed his wrist and pulled the spoon out of the bowl. "What's happened to your manners?"

Ian sat up indignantly. "Robin said I was guest of honor."

In his eagerness to defend himself, though, he held the spoon up almost vertically. Pork and beans began to ooze down the handle.

I grabbed his wrist and tilted the spoon back over the bowl. The last thing we needed was Mom scolding him for getting his shirt dirty. "The guest of honor has to wait for the toast," I said, quickly inventing an excuse.

Ian dropped the spoon into the bowl with a clank. "Toast?"

Dad picked up his beer. "Skoal."

I lifted my glass of ice water. "To the gamester. May your thumbs never wear out."

"To someone who's always a comfort," Mom said, raising her glass of water. I wondered if that was a dig at Dad and me.

We passed the bowl around, with Dad and Ian taking the bulk of the meal. When it finally came to me, I dished out two spoonfuls onto my plate.

"You really ought to take more, Robin," Mom said. Her own fork was halfway to her mouth.

I dished out two more spoonfuls and then tried to

change the subject. "Anything interesting happen at Gasser's today?" I asked Dad.

Dad finished chewing and swallowed elaborately. "I sold that expensive Pentax."

Mom tried to get involved. "Congratulations. You thought you'd never be able to find a buyer for it."

Dad looked surprised and then grateful. "He needed it, and he had the money, so it was a perfect match. How is it coming with Mad George's books?"

"It's a challenge," Mom said.

"If anyone can meet it, it's you," Dad said and smiled.

After a few minutes, Mom and Dad began to talk with the freedom and warmth of the old days. And listening to them, I could almost pretend things were now all right again for all of us.

Things were going so well, though, that Mom decided to push her luck. "Georgie has a script for a commercial he'd like to run on television."

Where Dad was concerned, that was like waving a red flag in front of a bull. "I don't do television."

"At least read it." Nervously Mom unfolded three typed pages that she had taken from the pocket of her blouse.

Dad grew more and more agitated as he flipped through them. "You, above all people, should object to seeing him in a coolie hat and pigtail." He glanced at a page and gave a snort. "Great Wall of bargains, indeed."

"We have to save our money for buying airtime on television," Mom said weakly. "Please. Won't you pitch in and help?"

Dad threw down the script. "Why do we have to keep sacrificing everything for your family? When do we get to think of ourselves?"

"Yes," I agreed. "Neither Nana nor Auntie Ann would ask us to give up everything and go work in their family business." Nana was Dad's mother and Auntie Ann was his sister. They both lived up in Chico.

Mom stared at me as if I'd just taken a knife and stabbed her in the back. "That's because they're not Chinese," Mom said.

Dad grinned gratefully at me. "In case you hadn't noticed it, we are in America."

"And the newspapers and television keep saying American families are falling apart," Mom argued unhappily. "I can give you plenty of examples of Chinese who are here and who make sacrifices to keep their families together." She began to tick them off on her fingers. "My friend Jane Lee waited to have children until after she had put all of her siblings through school. And Robin, look at Amy's mother. She works night and day . . ."

"Yes, dear," Dad said, putting an arm around me. "But what Robin and I want to know is when we can stop making sacrifices."

Mom looked at me, hurt. "I might have known you two would stick together."

"Maybe because Dad is right," I insisted.

"And because neither of you have your feet on the ground. You're both 'artistes.'" Mom sighed and waved a hand wildly in the air. "Both of you are always running off to chase after some artistic vision, and you leave the bills for someone else to pay. What's so wrong with making money for a change?"

"It's okay to dream, Elaine," Dad said, "and I pay my share of the bills."

Taking a deep breath, I put up my hands in the shape of a "T." "Hey, truce," I said.

Mom caught herself. "I tried to warn Georgie what you'd say. But I promised I'd ask."

She looked so miserable that Dad felt sorry for her. Stretching his hand over the table, he took Mom's hand.

"Well, I like going to Uncle Georgie's store," Ian declared.

"You're no help," I sighed.

Mom leaned to the side, holding out her arms until Ian slid off his seat and went to her. "You do like Uncle Georgie's store, don't you?" she asked.

"It's got a lot of neat things," Ian enthused as Mom's arms closed around him.

"It's all right to make people happy by helping them buy what they want, isn't it?" Mom asked.

"You're putting words into his mouth," Dad warned.

Ian, though, was nodding his head in agreement with what Mom had said. "Sure, it's nice to make people happy. It's nice to make money, too."

"At least you understand, don't you, darling?" Mom asked as she cuddled him.

Dad set his elbows on the table and cradled his head in his hands. "I've let you give away our privacy, and all your time. But you're not giving away my artistic integrity."

Mom let go of Ian. "Oh, is that what you call making documentaries no one wants to see," she snapped.

"This is supposed to be a family dinner," I said, "not a Godzilla movie."

"When you married me, you married my family," Mom insisted to Dad.

Ding. Round two.

"Make them stop," Ian whispered to me.

"I just tried to." Taking him by the hand, I pulled him from the chair. "We're finished with dinner, so may we be excused?"

Putting a hand behind his back, I nudged Ian away from the table, through the dining room, and down the hallway until we reached his bedroom. His lamp was still on, so it was easy to guide him to his bed. The Wolf Warrior pillowcases, sheets, and quilt made me smile despite everything. "You've got to be tough for just a little while longer. Uncle Georgie's business will take off, and Mom and Dad will straighten things out."

Sure, and I would dance *Swan Lake* with the American Ballet Theatre.

I forced myself to smile as I got him ready for bed. "Now go to sleep."

He rolled over onto one side and tried to cover up his ear with a spare pillow. "But I can still hear them."

I was afraid he'd suffocate. "You can't sleep like that," I said, grasping the upper pillow and gently pulling it free.

"Put the radio on, then." He pointed at his official Wolf Warrior radio.

"I'm sorry, but you heard Mrs. Aguilar complain. Your bedroom's right over theirs."

Ian looked up at me. "Then sing to me like you used to. You never do anymore."

"That's not true," I said, but I couldn't remember when I'd last sung. I guess when I had taken up ballet, I had concentrated on that and excluded everything else.

As Ian snuggled expectantly under the quilt, I got ready to sing softly. But for the life of me, I couldn't think of any lyrics. Not even the nursery ones. The only thing that came to mind was the cook's song, so I did that, singing it softly like a lullaby.

"I love a lady far away.
She never eats. She pines all day.
When she's asleep, she dreams of me—
The man who lives across the sea.

"Let's trade places, Madame Moon,
So I can see her very soon.
I'll touch her tears with my bright light
And make them pearls for her delight."

On the last line, I touched a fingertip to his cheek as if I, too, were making pearls.

After Ian blinked, he only managed to raise his eyelids halfway. "When did you start singing Chinese?" Ian knew Chinese better than I did.

"It's just something I heard today."

"From Grandmother?" he asked. He sounded almost jealous.

"No, in a restaurant." I tucked him in.

"Sing it again." He yawned and remembered his manners. "Please."

I was surprised that he wanted an encore, so I did. By the third time, he had fallen asleep.

I kissed him good night and tiptoed over the piles of his junk across the floor. I just wished there was someone to sing me to sleep.

As I opened his door, I heard Mom and Dad again. Quickly I crossed the hallway into my room, but even when I had shut my door, I didn't feel safe.

I couldn't understand why until I fell asleep. And suddenly I was out at Ocean Beach, building sand castles like I used to. Long after my parents had turned blue, I stayed out there making castles for myself.

Only this time, I was inside the castle. Outside I

could hear the tide pounding at my home. As I watched, the walls began to fall apart. Desperately, I snatched up handfuls of sand to patch them. Only I couldn't keep up. For every hole I filled, two more opened up. And through the gaping holes, I could see huge waves sweeping toward me. And I could do nothing.

NINE

To Wolf's House We Go

I hoped that things might be better when I woke up, but Monday morning began just the way Sunday had—with angry thunder rumbling from the next room. And it only got worse when they came home after work.

Ian took to hiding in his room during the rest of the week, and so did I. In the safety of my room, I would think about my fantasy family: of friendly Wolf, of my happy Grandmother . . . of me, safe and secure and loved.

I pictured us inside Wolf's kitchen, music playing on the radio while I danced and he cooked and Grandmother laughed. I imagined a lot of pleasant things—everything my life was not.

On Wednesday, Mom and Dad were arguing at dinner, so I was glad to leave the table when the phone rang.

"Robin, how are you?" It was Grandmother.

The receiver felt cool against my ear. "Okay. How are Uncle Georgie and Uncle Eddy?"

"They've been fighting all week. Your mother, too," Grandmother grumbled. "It's been as bad as when we were living in a single room in Hong Kong."

"Poor Mom," I said. She was carrying on a two-front war, with her brothers and with Dad. "And poor you."

"I feel more sorry for Wolf," Grandmother said. "At least we have a family."

"Such as it is," I said.

"He has all that sweetness dammed up inside, and no one to shower it on," Grandmother said. "Such a waste."

Monday and Tuesday's dinners had been burned to charcoal—or as Dad called them, "extra crispy." And tonight's had been scooped, unheated, out of tin cans. I found myself thinking longingly of the meal Wolf had made us. "And he was such a good cook."

"One of the best," Grandmother agreed.

It took a while for the truth to hit me—maybe because my brain was such a small target. I never stopped to think that my poor grandmother, trapped among her quarreling children, also might have been fantasizing about a safe haven in the Celestial Forest.

Well, why not? It would be nice to escape the arguing for a few hours. And if we went together, we'd be safe enough.

With growing excitement, I asked, "By the way, have you thought any more about this Saturday?"

"Have you?" she asked. She was trying hard to keep her voice neutral, but I could hear the hopefulness creep in.

"Well," I said, playing with the telephone cord, "he seemed eager for us to come back."

"And we can't discard the poor man like a facial tissue," Grandmother rationalized.

She must have been as sick of our real family as I was.

"Why not do another good deed?" I asked.

Grandmother's voice grew almost chipper. "It would be the right thing to do."

I couldn't help smiling. "Do you think the store can spare you?"

"I'm so busy with the store," Grandmother said slowly. "But I might be able to squeeze out some free time."

"I think I might have some time," I said.

"Then perhaps we should go," she said and lowered her voice so that it was soft yet bubbly—like that of a small girl planning some prank. "But we don't need to tell anyone, do we?"

It would be our little secret. "Of course not."

That next Saturday at practice, I paid close attention to Madame's instructions. When we had the actual recital, I didn't intend to fall on my backside as I had in Wolf's kitchen.

When practice was over, my feet were sore and every muscle seemed to ache. Madame had worked all of us hard. Yet, even though I was tired, I had a date with Grandmother, so I hurried to the store. Grand-mother was waiting in her red cloth coat as she sat behind a counter, impatiently tapping a foot. On either side of her, Uncle Georgie and Uncle Eddy were quarreling, so she was in the middle of a stereophonic battle.

Grandmother immediately rose on her canes when she saw me. "Robin, over here." Then she rapped a cane on the glass top of the counter until her sons were quiet. "Call me a cab. Robin and I want to leave now," she said to them.

"Where are you going, Mama?" Uncle Georgie demanded, suddenly curious.

"We have . . . friends in Chinatown," Grandmother began to make her way from behind the counter.

Uncle Eddy was just as inquisitive. "Who?"

Grandmother rapped her cane imperiously, one, two. "I am not your child. I do not have to tell you."

Both her sons were taken aback by her angry reaction. "Okay, okay," Uncle Eddy soothed, "just don't break the counter."

Obviously dying to know more, Uncle Georgie dialed up a taxi, and then he and his brother waited silently with us. At least, their curiosity forged a temporary truce between the two of them.

When the cab arrived, Grandmother told the cabby to take us to the Celestial Forest in Chinatown and gave him the address. As we settled back against the vinyl seats, I asked, "What about Ah Wing?"

Grandmother poked my elbow. "It might lead to too many questions if we had our own personal chauffeur."

I eyed her suspiciously. "For a grandmother, you're awfully good at conspiracies."

She squirmed, trying to change the subject. "And how is Madame? I haven't been able to shop with her since the store opened." Grandmother and my ballet teacher were special friends, and though Madame had been born in Russia and later danced in Europe, she was an old hand at American ways and often interpreted life in America for Grandmother.

I shrugged. "Okay."

Grandmother sighed. "I miss going to garage sales with her."

"She doesn't have much time on Saturdays between class and practice for the recital," I said.

"And usually I have to be at the store," Grandmother said mournfully.

While Grandmother sat contemplating all the treasures that had been lost to her, I looked out the cab window. I could feel myself growing excited as we headed into Chinatown again. I had been there before with my parents, but my mother was always in too much of a hurry to explain things. So up until my visits with Grandmother, Chinatown and its inhabitants had always been something to look at. Like fish in a glass aquarium. Close enough to touch and yet separate. Self-contained. I think that's why more than anything, I didn't think of myself as being particularly Chinese. But now with Grandmother's help I could enter that world.

However, when we got to Chinatown, there wasn't much that seemed fairy-tale-like about it. In fact, it was the busiest I had ever seen it. I thought Clement Street in the Richmond District was pretty crowded on weekends, but the streets here were twice as bad. There were shoppers with bulging bags everywhere, and trucks unloading crates of vegetables and even whole sides of beef. The cab just crawled along in the thick traffic.

As we slowly passed a fish store, I saw how jammed the aisles were. A lady brushed past a pan of crabs, and one of the crabs nipped her.

She jumped and turned. Using some Chinese Grandmother had as yet to teach me, she slapped the nearest man.

"At least you know the crabs are fresh," Grandmother said and patted the back of the front seat. "Here, driver," she said.

He pulled over in front of the Celestial Forest. As she paid him, the cars began to pile up behind us and honk their horns. Rather than annoy Grandmother, the angry noise seemed to invigorate her. "Just like Hong Kong," she grinned.

We got out carefully, making our way single-file between two parked automobiles. Despite having to lean on two canes, Grandmother didn't seem bothered in the least by the crowded sidewalks. In fact, the mob seemed to excite her. "Yes, it's just like Hong Kong," she beamed.

As she dodged nimbly around a group of gossiping Chinese women, I shook my head in admiration. "Where did you learn moves like that?"

Grandmother blinked at me. "What moves?"

"It's too bad you can't skate." I had to laugh. "You'd be a star at roller derby."

"I'm too old to learn," Grandmother groaned.

"You're never too old," I said in alarm. She had never talked like this before.

"It's the store making me old," Grandmother grumbled. "I need to get to Chinatown more often."

"Do you miss Hong Kong still?" I asked her sympathetically.

Grandmother glanced over her shoulder at me as she led me through the mob. "You won't tell your mother?"

"I won't," I promised.

"Yes, you will," she said, sliding around a woman whose baby hung from a sling on her back. "You can't keep any secrets from your mother."

"I swear," I said. "Not even if she tortures me."

Grandmother scrutinized me and seemed to reach some decision. "Well, yes, I do miss Hong Kong. There's no city like it. And there never will be again."

Ah Wing greeted us at the entrance to the Celestial Forest. "Why didn't you call me?" he scolded.

"We didn't want to bother you," Grandmother said. "Did you win?"

"Naw. It's up to forty-three million now. It'll be even better when we win this one," he said, stepping away from the door so she could come in.

When I followed Grandmother into the crowded restaurant, a wave of noise rolled over me—the old men joking, teasing, arguing, and reminiscing, all at full volume.

The waiter turned toward us with a couple of menus in one hand and a pot of tea in the other. "You did come back," he said in surprise.

"We didn't say we wouldn't," Grandmother said.

T E N

Lost Boys

The customers stared at us and began to whisper and point as I helped Grandmother take her coat off. I was surprised to see her wearing her best blue satin dress. "Well, look who's gotten all fancy," I teased. I had pulled on sweats over my practice outfit.

"After all, I am the wife of an artist," she said proudly.

Wolf bustled eagerly out of the kitchen. He had on a white shirt under his apron. "Today you won't be able to resist my cooking," he promised.

I was pleased that I couldn't smell liquor on his breath this time. Maybe we'd gotten him to stop drinking. So perhaps we really were doing some good after all.

"We're ready," Grandmother said with a smile.

As Wolf marched into his kitchen, the waiter unfolded a tablecloth and spread it over the table. "Real linen," he boasted as he folded two napkins. "I used to work on the *Queen Elizabeth*. That's a big boat. Margaret Truman loved the roses I cut out of raw potatoes for decoration." With a few deft twists of his hands, he folded the napkins into swans and set them before us.

A man in a red windbreaker turned around. "Hey," he complained mock-seriously, "how come they get those, and all we get is these lousy paper ones?"

"Because they won't steal theirs like you do, Ah Bock," the waiter snapped.

At each place, he set plastic chopsticks, a plate, a bowl and a soup spoon.

When Wolf brought out the first course, people stood up around the restaurant trying to see what it was.

"Shark fin soup," Wolf announced and set it down before us. The tureen matched our soup bowls. Then, with one hand behind his back, he ladled out the soup.

Of course, the customers had to get involved again. "Hey, little girl," Ah Wing said, "you know how fishermen get the shark fins?"

I had been enjoying just sniffing the aromas.

"No, sir," I said politely. "How?"

"They hook the shark by its mouth and hold it in their right hand while they cut off its fin with their left." Ah Wing held up his right arm. He had pulled his hand within the sleeve itself. "That's why all the shark fishermen are called Lefty." He chuckled at his own joke. "Get it?" he asked me.

"How awful," I blurted out.

That only made Ah Wing guffaw. He looked around at the other customers. "She thinks it's awful." They started to roar.

With the ladle still in his hand, Wolf shifted his feet as if he were embarrassed.

"I . . . I should work on the next course." He left hurriedly, trailing soup behind him from the dripping ladle.

Had I spoiled the illusion for him? At least in ballet, I had some notion of what I was doing. But when it came to acting like a Chinese girl, I realized that I knew nothing at all. I had been so busy imagining our happy time in the kitchen that I had not considered what would happen when we stepped outside.

"Go on, eat," Ah Wing urged. He turned to the other regulars and waved his hands like a cheerleader. Right away they began to chant, "Eat, eat."

Grandmother could see me squirming. "Just pretend you're on stage and they're your audience," she whispered.

I guess I was in the spotlight in a way. "Dancing's different from eating," I said. I couldn't help glancing around out of the corners of my eyes. The whole restaurant was watching my every bite.

"Don't mind them." Grandmother leaned forward as she continued to talk in a low voice. "Remember what I told you? Most of the men here came over from

China as boys. They didn't have their mothers or sisters around, only other boys and men."

I used the spoon to play idly with my soup. "So they were away from their families for most of their lives." That made me feel sad again.

"They never really had a chance to grow up inside," Grandmother explained. "Did you ever read *Peter Pan?*"

"No, but I saw the movie," I said.

"Well, these men are a lot like Peter Pan's Lost Boys," Grandmother explained.

That made sense. Ah Wing had made the kind of joke that Ian and small boys would laugh at. Though they were grown men, they reminded me of the boys at school. In fact, emotionally a lot of them didn't seem much older than Ian. Their insults were like fake punches, and their tough talk was really just play.

"And maybe Wolf is their Peter Pan," I said slowly.

It made me feel even sadder—and a little scared, too, at whom I was dealing with. Maybe that was how Wendy had felt when she first met the Lost Boys.

I dipped my spoon into the bowl. The soup tasted wonderful to me, but then I'd never had it before. So I consulted a real authority. "How is it?" I asked Grandmother.

"Some of the best I've ever had," she said, slurping noisily.

The chanting had stopped with my first spoonful, and now that I knew the soup had her stamp of approval, I happily went on eating. And then I had another bowl, because it seemed to be mostly broth and protein.

"She likes it," Ah Bock said, giving the thumbs-up, and around the restaurant I saw heads nod in satisfaction.

They must have been more than casual customers. I could only guess that word had spread among Wolf's regulars and friends, and they had packed the room this afternoon. It was humbling to realize that our visit meant so much to Wolf.

When the soup was down to the dregs, Grandmother used her chopsticks to pick out tidbits. When there were only a couple of spoonfuls of broth left, the waiter came to fetch the tureen away. "Well, Wolf will be pleased."

I hoped so. Maybe that would make up for my earlier flub. "That was delicious," I said, as I dabbed my mouth with the napkin. I was hoping I could stave off the rest of the banquet, but I had no luck.

"You can't stop him now. It'd be like trying to stop a runaway train." The waiter took away the big soup tureen, but left the two soup bowls.

With considerable pomp, the waiter came back to us. "Peking duck," he said and put it down on the table. "Do you want me to show you how to eat it?"

"No, thank you." I'd had Peking duck before. As it cooks, the skin separates from the body—which leaves it crisp and crunchy. I pulled apart one of the little buns and added some of the duck meat and part of the skin before I added some of the special plum sauce the waiter had set out in small dishes. It tasted heavenly.

"Hey," Ah Bock complained to the waiter, "how come that isn't on the menu either?"

"Because this is a labor of love," the waiter snapped as he filled our empty soup bowls with rice.

"But she's hardly eating any of it," Ah Bock complained.

Ah Wing reached over and patted Ah Bock on his belly. "It's not like you need to eat any more."

"What's wrong?" the waiter whispered. "Do you want money?"

"It's not that," I said, shaking my head. I didn't know how to explain about there being no such thing as fat ballerinas. My ignorance made me feel like I had just been shoved onto a stage and told to dance without any practice or knowing what the steps were.

"Eat, eat," Ah Bock said. Turning, he waved his hand, orchestrating the chant from the others.

It would have been hard enough to have a regular audience studying my every bite, but it was even harder in front of these overgrown Lost Boys.

My ears burning with embarrassment, I tried to make the bun last by nibbling slowly and chewing thoroughly, but all too soon I'd finished it. "Take another bun," Grandmother urged.

"I can't," I said miserably.

After the soup, there were four more courses, and each tasted better than the last. It took an almost superhuman effort to keep from eating more than a few bites of each.

Finally, Wolf strolled out of his kitchen, wiping his hands on a towel. His hair was matted to his head with perspiration as if he had just danced all the roles in *Swan Lake*.

I was dreading this moment.

He looked distressed when he saw all the platters still almost full. "You've hardly touched a thing. What's the matter? Didn't you like it?"

What had ever made me think I could pass as a Chinese daughter? When I had come down here, I had been thinking only of myself. The last thing I wanted to do was hurt his feelings: Unfortunately, in his eyes eating big was beautiful.

"It was wonderful," I said. "I ate more than I usually do." In fact, I would have to go over to my friend Leah's and use her practice room to work off some of today's lunch.

"You really should eat more," Wolf said, eyeing me critically. "You're just skin and bones. We need to fatten you up."

"But it's all muscle," I said and proudly raised an arm, bending it at the elbow. "That's from dancing."

Behind Wolf's back, I saw the waiter shake his head,

and Ah Bock at the next table laughed. "She looks like a field hand."

Too late, I realized that I'd made another mistake. It's an awful thing to screw up your real life. It's even worse to screw up your fantasy life.

The laughter rose around me like giant walls. I felt like I was at the bottom of a pit with no way out.

I looked desperately toward the front door, wanting only to escape this disaster.

ELEVEN

The Martian

Wolf sprang to my defense. "You keep your opinions to yourself," he scolded Ah Bock with a lift of his head, "or I'll burn every dish you order."

Ah Bock took that as the ultimate threat. He hunched his shoulders as he said, "Sorry, sorry."

Ah Wing swaggered over to the loud man and slapped him on the arm. "What would you know about girls anyway, Ah Bock? You haven't spoken to a female for twenty years."

As the others cackled with laughter, Ah Bock countered, "And what do you call my wife?"

"I don't know," Ah Wing snickered. "What do you?"

Ah Bock rubbed the back of his head sheepishly. That joke had everyone practically rolling on the floor.

In fact, the laughter was so loud that Wolf had to wait for things to quiet down before he wagged an index finger at me. "You really should eat more."

"We've explained her reasons," Grandmother said protectively.

It was Wolf's turn to look lost—as if he had dropped his compass. "I'm sorry." This hadn't been part of his plan for the afternoon. Guiltily, I realized that I was spoiling everything.

"I know what will tempt you." He reached under his apron into his shirt pocket. "I've been asking some of my friends about what children like," he said as his hand wriggled around inside the pocket.

I was touched that he had been researching his role as a father. I realized that I should have been researching mine.

"Here you go," he said triumphantly. Behind him, Ah Bock put up his thumb.

When I looked up into Wolf's face, I saw such an eagerness to please me. But when I looked at his outstretched palm, I saw Wolf Warrior Treats. They were almost pure sugar with a little chocolate thrown in for flavoring. Too bad Ian wasn't around. He would have stuffed all of them into his mouth at once.

It made me feel utterly miserable that I couldn't eat the treats. I glanced helplessly at Grandmother. She tried to save the awkward situation by stretching out her hand. "Thank you," she said as she began to unwrap one of them.

Wolf looked puzzled as he waved the rest of the treats at me. "How about you? Sweets for the sweet?"

His joke sounded almost rehearsed, as if he had been planning out bits of conversation for the last week. I couldn't remember when my parents had gone to so much trouble over me.

"No, thank you," I said, trying to smile.

"What's wrong?" Ah Bock demanded. "My grand-kids love those."

Wolf curled his fingers up over the treats. "How old are your grandchildren anyway, Ah Bock?"

Ah Bock scratched the back of his neck. "I don't know. The wife knows that stuff."

Wolf planted a fist upon Ah Bock's table. "Well, what grade are they in?"

"They haven't started to school yet," Ah Bock ad-mitted.

"Can't you see she's almost a young woman?" Wolf's face turned a mottled red. He looked ready to fling the candies at Ah Bock, but with great effort he merely set them down on the table before him. "Here. Give these to them then." Then he turned back to me. "I'm so sorry. I didn't mean any insult."

It was an awkward moment for both of us. "You were trying to do something nice. Thank you," I said.

Still ashamed, Wolf wiped his hands. "It's so hard. I mean, I didn't know." If he had been over here while his daughter had been growing up in China, he wouldn't have had much practice at being a father.

Grandmother came to our rescue again by getting

him to reminisce. "In the old days, we didn't take food for granted, did we?"

"Back home we were lucky to get anything to eat," Wolf agreed.

Grandmother nodded. "It was hard back there."

Wolf pantomimed a backhand. "If you were fussy about your food, Mother gave you a good whack. And then fed your dinner to the pig."

Grandmother played along. "Oh, yes. We did the same thing with our pig."

"Big black spot on the back." Wolf spread his hands to indicate the size. "Mother never let us name him because we were going to eat him when he matured." He chuckled. "I remember one day Mother chopped up some bean curd and vegetables. She'd laid out everything nice and neat. And then she turned her back. Before you could blink an eye, that pig scooted in, stood up on its hind legs, and gobbled up half of everything."

"Did he make it to maturity?" Grandmother asked.

"Of course. He was our wedding feast," Wolf chuckled.

"Oh yes, I forgot," Grandmother said.

"Sometimes I can't remember, either," Wolf smiled. "It's all like a dream."

And he went on talking about his village. It sat on a hillside overlooking a fertile valley. At the mouth of the valley was the tiger-shaped rock that had given the village its name.

Grandmother knew enough of life in a rural village to draw out more of a description of the village. It didn't sound like such a bad place—if you didn't mind it being quiet. Small rice fields were scattered across the floor of the valley like the patches of a quilt. And terraced fields were planted on the "hillsides," where the soil was sandier. There the villagers grew small, sweet yams.

Wolf and Grandmother talked until I could picture the village with its green-tiled roofs, drowsing on the hillside. The water chain rattling as its belt of small bamboo buckets fed water to the fields from the stream. Ducks wandering along the side of a field, probing in the mud for bugs.

I thought it must be nice for Grandmother to have someone to talk to about that stuff, but I felt more alien than ever—as if I had just been dropped on Mars.

I was such a bust as Wolf's daughter that my only solution was to flee. "We should be going," I said to Grandmother.

Wolf stood awkwardly next to our table for a moment as if he wanted to say more.

"We really should," Grandmother said.

Wolf nodded to Ah Wing, who jumped up from his table. "I'll get my cab," he volunteered and headed for the door.

"Let me get my coat, and I'll wait with you outside," Wolf said.

As soon as he disappeared into his kitchen, Ah

Bock shook his head. "You're crazy, you know? At a fancy Chinatown place, a meal like this would cost you fifty, sixty dollars," he chided me.

Curiosity got the better of me. "Why doesn't he cook at one of the ritzy places then?"

The waiter put cartons and a pink plastic bag on the table. "Because their owners don't understand."

Ah Bock pantomimed drinking something. "You know. They think he drinks too much."

"You can't cook in a worse place than here." The waiter regarded Ah Bock sourly. "Or for worse customers."

If this had been a course in being Chinese, I would have flunked the test. Determined to perform better as the daughter, I grabbed the arm of the waiter as he started to fill the cartons. "I'm doing a lousy job as his daughter," I said in English. "You've got to give me more info."

The waiter gazed at my hand as if it were a scab that mysteriously had appeared on his arm. He didn't speak until I let go. "Like what?"

Where to begin? "For starters, where are we supposed to be from?"

"Tiger Rock village, Toisan," the waiter said as he dumped the buns into a small carton.

I glanced at Grandmother. For my sake, she explained, "Toisan is the district in southern China that most Chinese-Americans are from."

"Satisfied? I've got work to do." The waiter tried to pull away.

"What's his name?" Grandmother asked. "I mean, his formal name."

The waiter rolled his eyes. "Yee Golden-Promise."

"And mine?" I asked.

"Yee Winter-Flower." And he turned to Grandmother. "And you're Spring-Pearl. May I go now? I've got other customers."

"Spring-Pearl," Grandmother said slowly, as if chewing on the name.

I sat back to think about my name, too. Yee Winter-Flower. "So maybe I'm something rare like a flower in the snow. Or maybe even a snowflake."

"No," Grandmother said. "Wolf comes from southern China. There's no snow there, and flowers bloom all year round."

By the time the waiter had boxed all the goodies and put them into the bag, Wolf had come out in a jacket.

When we stepped outside, the fog was drifting in wisps down the hills of Chinatown. In the twilight, they floated like drifting down toward the bay.

"Don't catch cold," he said, pulling up the collar on my jacket. He looked down at me solicitously. He should have been doing this for his real little girl, I thought, and that made me ache inside.

Suddenly, down the street, a car horn tooted and headlights flashed. The next moment, a cab had pulled away from the curb and into the traffic. I started to wave. "Here," I said.

I held up the bag of goodies for Ah Wing. "Same price as last time?"

He licked his chops. "Deal."

Wolf hurried forward to open the door to the backseat. "Will I see you next week at about the same time?"

Grandmother glanced at me as she got in. Funny, but she made me feel almost as if I were her chaperone. "If we can."

From her look, I guessed it all depended on my accompanying her. But I didn't know if I wanted to go through another afternoon of flubbing my lines. "We'll try," I said, sliding in after her.

"Don't be mad at me. Please come next Saturday," Wolf begged. "I promise that I'll do better next time." Surprised, I whirled around in my seat, but he had already closed the door.

"What do you mean?" I asked.

He couldn't hear me through the shut door, though, and before I could roll the window down, Ah Wing had started forward.

Helplessly, I watched him stand there, waving goodbye, as we left him behind.

TWELVE

Moon Dance

As Ah Wing's taxi chugged up the steep hill out of Chinatown, I sank back into the worn vinyl seat.

"I blew it bad," I said.

Grandmother patted my knee. "You were fine."

I shook my head and refused to be consoled. "I should have been prepared. I made a fool out of myself."

Grandmother shifted the purse on her lap. "I'm the one who's the fool. I babbled on and on about the 'good old days.' " She looked so sad that I felt guilty. There I was feeling sorry for myself when I should have been thinking about her.

I twisted around on the seat. "No, I think that was the most fun part for him. He liked talking about the past."

Grandmother pursed her lips. "Do you think so?"

"He looked so happy when you were talking about the pig," I assured her.

It wasn't like Grandmother to be uncertain about anything. She had opinions about everything, and they came in black-and-white only and with clearly defined edges. However, she began to open and close the clasp of her purse with crisp snaps. "You're not just saying that to make me feel good?"

Ah Wing cleared his throat. "I've never seen him talk so much. Usually all he does is grunt. But then he is drunk most of the time. Not today—thanks to you."

"You like Wolf, don't you?" Grandmother asked thoughtfully.

"He's gotten a real raw deal out of life. Me, I'm just a bum. I don't deserve more than this beat-up old jalopy." He indicated his taxi with a wave of his hand. "But he ought to be cooking in some fine, big restaurant for rich gourmets who can appreciate his stuff."

I couldn't resist nudging Grandmother. "Are you a little sweet on Wolf?"

I should have known better. Grandmother hated to talk about herself. "Don't be ridiculous," she huffed. "I'm much too busy with the store to have time for that nonsense."

I thought of what the store had done to Mom and Dad. "I'm sick of that store."

"The family comes first," Grandmother declared.

"You've made enough sacrifices for your family. When does it stop?" I asked.

"Never," Grandmother insisted.

"But—"

Grandmother folded her arms. "Besides, I'm much too old for that sort of thing."

"You're not that old," Ah Wing said. "In fact, everyone says you're quite a handsome woman."

In the fading light, I would have sworn Grandmother was blushing. "You only think that because you're practically ancient."

"Old White Whiskers, that's me," Ah Wing agreed cheerfully. "The only thing older than my taxi is me."

Grandmother started to chuckle, and I was grateful that he had managed to lift her spirits. Opening her purse, she took out the two dollar bills and dangled them over the back of the front seat. "Well, White Whiskers, what numbers should we play this week?"

He used the rear-view mirror to guide his fingers to the money. "Chinese dates or American dates?"

"Aren't they the same?" I asked.

He tucked the money into his jacket pocket. "Naw, you Americans use the sun for your calendar and we Chinese use the moon."

Grandmother rapped the back of Ah Wing's head with a knuckle. "She's Chinese, too," she said, smiling at me. "Very Chinese."

Ah Wing was amused. "She doesn't gamble."

She poked me in the arm. "She's thrifty like her grandmother."

As they discussed their financial strategies, I remembered Wolf's last words. Maybe he thought he was the one who had fallen on stage as he pretended to be my father. He was so considerate.

Then I began to think about the meal in the restaurant—not as a fantasy but as a performance, and I thought about what Madame had taught me to do if I made a mistake during a performance.

In the Celestial Forest today, I hadn't just fallen like I had that first time in the kitchen. This time I had done the equivalent of belly flopping right off the stage. I made a promise to myself right then and there that I would be prepared next week if Grandmother went to Chinatown—and I was sure she would.

And in my own small way, I'd try to make up for the lousy hand Wolf had been dealt: For a couple of hours, I would make his daughter come back to life.

Ah Wing was watching Grandmother in his rear-view mirror. "So how many years have you been here?"

"Just one," Grandmother said, holding up an index finger.

"China-born, huh?" Ah Wing asked thoughtfully.

"How long have you been here?" Grandmother asked.

Reflected in the rear-view mirror, Ah Wing's forehead creased in thought. "Fifty-eight years. My old man brought me here when I was eight. But I don't know that I consider it a lucky number."

"You've had hard times?" Grandmother asked sympathetically.

"Well, I've had those," he admitted. "But mostly I never met the right woman. The ones born here were too bossy—no insult intended," he added to me. "And by the time I thought of finding one at home, I couldn't. Revolutions, wars . . ." He shrugged as if he didn't want to elaborate.

He didn't talk any more, and Grandmother didn't try to continue the conversation. Instead, she just stared out the window at the passing street. I wondered what she was thinking about? Maybe Wolf?

This time Grandmother had told Ah Wing to take us to her apartment. She lived with Uncle Eddy, or to be more precise, she lived under him. Auntie Marilyn, Uncle Eddy's wife, had not gotten along with Grandmother when she first moved in with them. Fortunately, they had a small apartment on the ground floor, next to their garage. The L-shaped apartment had a small kitchen, bathroom, and bedroom. So Uncle Eddy had wound up evicting his tenant and moving Grandmother down there. It was an arrangement that suited everybody—except on the nights when Grandmother played her Chinese opera records too loud. Uncle Eddy's house was a large green building squeezed into the middle of its block. Except for the color and some of the trimming details on the roof, it looked exactly like hundreds of other houses in the Richmond District. It was basically the same kind of building as our flat, but it had only one front door and an alley on the right side.

The cabby was driving slowly, craning his neck to see the address numbers, and pulled in to the curb near Uncle Eddy's.

"This is it," Grandmother said, pointing at her home.

"Next Saturday, you call me," Ah Wing urged, patting the pocket that held her two dollars. "We're partners now."

"I will," Grandmother said.

We climbed out of the taxi onto the sidewalk, and as Ah Wing drove away, she lifted a cane. "Make us rich," she called.

Now that Ah Wing was gone, I could try to pry again. "So, do you like Wolf?"

Grandmother snorted. "At my age, I like comfortable slippers."

"But—"

"You've been watching too many soap operas," Grandmother snapped.

As I helped her inside, I tried again to get her to talk, but she got huffy, practically shoving me out the door.

Our flat was only six blocks from Grandmother's apartment. All the way home, I couldn't shake off a sad feeling. It could have been Grandmother. My parents. Wolf and his family. Any and all of them. I felt saturated in it—like a piece of cloth soaked with tears.

When I got to our front door, I saw a small shadowy bundle on the steps. I approached it cautiously because there had been some muggings in the area lately. More than likely it was some poor homeless person sleeping on our steps—it had been happening more and more often.

Suddenly, the dark shape lifted its head. "It's about time you got home, Robin." I saw Ian's face. There was a dirty stripe on either cheek, running from eye down to chin.

I sat down beside him. "Did someone hit you?"

"No." Ian wiped clumsily at his eyes with a sleeve, and I realized he was in his pajamas. Ian seemed so small and helpless. I put my arm around him. "What're you doing out here?"

"Reading comic books." On his other side, lying in the pool of light cast by the streetlamp, I saw a half-dozen of his Wolf Warrior comics.

I could hear Mom and Dad's voices even from here. They were too faint to make out the words, but the tone was clear: dark and ugly and angry. I sat holding Ian for a moment, feeling just as scared and angry as he did—as if a vandal had thrown paint on a family portrait.

I wanted in the worst way to go to Grandmother's but I didn't want to add to her worries. There was no place else to go. "Come on," I said, kissing the top of Ian's head. He smelled of soap. Someone, probably Mom, had gotten him to bathe today. "We can't stay out here all night."

Sometimes it was easy to forget how young Ian was.

"I guess not," he sighed and straightened. He collected his comic books calmly, as if he were gathering his homework from a desk. Then he stood up on the step. "Let's go inside."

Ian put his free hand into mine. Together we mounted the steps into the dark at the top of the stairs, guided more by memory than by vision. While I fumbled for my keys, Ian pushed the front door and it swung open.

"We each have to do our share," Mom was saying. "We can't afford to hire a director."

"Why do we have to keep sacrificing everything for your family? When do we get to think of ourselves?" Dad responded.

It was the same old argument. I kicked the door shut with my heel, hoping that the noise would remind Dad and Mom that they had an audience. But their angry voices continued to roll toward us. "He's my brother, Gil," Mom reminded Dad. "Love me, love him. My family and I come as a package. You knew what you were getting into when you married me."

"Come on," I whispered to Ian. I had to pull him through the door, clutching his comics under his arm. Then I nudged him down the hallway until we reached his bedroom. I kissed him. "You've got to be tough for just a little while longer."

"You promise things will get better?"

"Yes." I wondered how I could ever keep that promise, though. "Now go to sleep," I said and left.

Though the lights weren't on in my room, it seemed very bright. I put up the shade on my window and saw that the moon had risen. Full and round, the disk flooded my room with a silvery light.

Through the door, I could hear my parents still arguing. As I stared up at the moon, I could hear Wolf's light, quavery voice again as he sang his sad little tune. How many other people had wished they could trade places with the moon? If I could, I would escape all the fighting, all the anger, all the frustration down here.

I felt so sad I could burst. Wolf's song haunted me, and I began to hum it. One foot started to tap, and then the other. It always happened with music I liked. Madame called it kinetic pleasure. I couldn't enjoy a tune just by listening to it with my ears. My whole body had to get involved, and I began dancing my solitary dance for the moon, hoping she was looking down and could see me.

THIRTEEN

Daughterhood 101

On Sunday morning, my parents and Ian were gone early again. So I just stayed in bed daydreaming. Ian could escape into his video games. I had my fantasy with Grandmother.

I liked having a secret life. It gave me a private place to hide when the storms were raging. In China what would we have done as a family? How would we have lived? Perhaps we would have had a nice little cottage by a river where we could picnic. Wolf and Grandmother would have sung to each other, and I would have danced to their songs.

But what would I have looked like? Curious, I got up and poked my head out into the hallway. "Hello?"

When I didn't get any answer, I thought it was safe to sneak into my parents' bedroom.

Their closet door was closed, but I opened it and looked along the rack of clothes until I found Mom's high-collared Chinese coat. Taking it off the pole, I went into the bathroom, where I braided my hair like the girls in Chinese movies. But I had brown hair and green eyes just like Dad's. The only thing Chinese about my reflection was the coat.

I studied myself from several angles, but in no way did I look Chinese. What about me could possibly remind the cook of his daughter?

Or maybe really being Chinese didn't depend on how you looked. Just like being Jewish didn't depend on your having any one set of features. I knew I was half Chinese whether anyone recognized it or not. In fact, I felt Chinese—though I couldn't have told you what about me was specifically Chinese.

It was more than a familiarity with chopsticks and Chinese food and the lingo. And it was more than feeling comfortable—I had found out yesterday there was so much I did not understand. Somehow, though, the cook had connected with the Chinese part of me.

I had to admit to myself that Wolf could have been just plain desperate. There had been all this love, all this caring dammed up inside him until he had been ready to explode. And when he finally had an outlet, the love just poured over Grandmother and me. If that was being crazy, then maybe we all should be.

Taking off Mom's coat, I returned it to her closet. Maybe there wasn't anything I could do about my real family, but I could work on my fantasy one. Pleasing

Wolf meant pleasing Grandmother as well as myself. And who knows? If I could find out how to succeed with my fantasy family, maybe I could apply the lessons to my real one.

First things first, though: I had to pass as a Chinese daughter. That meant learning everything I could about being one. The next time I went to Chinatown, the Lost Boys would have to find someone or something else to laugh about, and I would do nothing that would upset Wolf. I'd correct my mistakes just as I had with my Red Riding Hood dance. First, practice the basics and then memorize the steps.

But I didn't know the most fundamental things about being a Chinese daughter. How was I going to learn? Asking Mom was too risky. The only other "dutiful daughter" that I knew was Amy.

When I called her, I could hear her brothers and sisters yelling in the background. "One of the brats is sick. So I'm stuck inside with them all," Amy sighed. Since her mother had gone to work as a nanny for a rich family, Amy always had to babysit at home.

"That was some practice yesterday," I said. "Are you still aching?"

"Always," she said.

We talked a while before I got around to the point of the phone call. "Amy, do you remember anything about your father?" I asked.

"Not much," Amy said. "He died five years ago."

"But if he'd lived, what kinds of things would you have to do?" I asked. "I mean, as a dutiful Chinese daughter."

"But your dad's American," Amy said to me.

Though Amy was one of my best friends, I couldn't tell her about my Chinatown family. That was too fragile a fantasy to share with anyone else yet. "I'm just . . . just curious."

But Amy started to shout at a brother who was jumping on the sofa. When she came on the line again, she sounded agitated. "I really shouldn't talk anymore. My mom's still at work, and the runts are going wild. Can't you ask your cousins?"

"My cousins are too . . . well, Americanized," I said. Uncle Georgie's and Uncle Eddy's kids knew even less about being Chinese than I did.

"What about your friends in Chinatown?" she asked.

To my chagrin I had to admit that I had no friends in Chinatown. "All my Chinese friends are out here, and none of them seem . . . uh . . . traditional. And none of them know as much as you."

"It's not as if I took lessons," she warned me. "It's just something I grew up with."

I was surprised at how I felt inside. The need to know was almost physical—like a hunger. "Please help me."

Some kid was crying, and I waited for Amy to

soothe her. "Be glad you're not a slave," Amy sighed. "You don't have to babysit your brothers and sisters night and day, or cook all three meals, or clean the house, or do the laundry."

I felt as if I had dialed the wrong number. "Sorry to bother you," I said hastily.

Amy realized she was overwhelming me. "It feels good to get it out. Thanks."

I tried to sound breezy. "What are friends for?"

It was quiet at the other end of the line, though. "So you'd really like to know what it's like to be Chinese?"

"Yeah, I guess I would."

Amy spoke slowly as she thought. She did the same thing when we worked on a math problem together. "I guess you'd be quiet. No arguing. No contradicting." She chuckled. "You wouldn't survive more than ten minutes."

She was probably right, if I had to act that way all the time, but on my short visits to the cook it would be possible. I began to take notes on a pad. "What else?"

"You'd be attentive," she said. "Father's are masters of the household. If he wanted a glass of water, you'd get it for him—except he'd probably want hot tea." She added, "But you know what the hardest part of being a Chinese daughter is?"

I barely heard her voice over the loud noise in the background. "No, what?" I asked cautiously.

"Getting away from my responsibilities and finding time for friends like you," she said.

That sounded like my old Amy. "Thanks," I said. "If I wanted to find out more about a Chinese family, how would I do that? I mean, if they were dead?"

Amy was puzzled. "I guess I'd talk to their family."

Wolf was the only member of his family I knew. "I couldn't do that."

"Well, you could try his or her family association," Amy suggested. "Some Chinese are organized by their family names. For instance, my name is Chin so I belong to the Chin family association."

I thought of my own family. "But my mother doesn't belong to an association."

"I should correct myself." Amy said. "The Chinese who come from southern China are organized by family associations. The Chinese who come from Hong Kong or Taiwan don't necessarily belong to those associations."

It was worth a try. "Thanks," I said.

"Sure," Amy said. "What are friends for?"

I would have liked to ask more, but it sounded like World War III was about to break out at her house, so I let her go.

As soon as I hung up, I went straight to the phone book. Sure enough, there was a Yee family association. I wrote down the number, then picked up the receiver and poked at the tiny buttons. On the third ring, someone answered. "Hello?" a man said in English.

"Yee family association?" I asked.

"No speak," the man said brusquely.

I wondered why he had answered in English then, but I switched to Chinese. "I'm looking for the Yee family association."

"This is the place. What do you want?" the man demanded impatiently in Chinese.

At first, I didn't understand his lack of friendliness. After all, what about any lost Yees in America who might be seeking help from their clan? However, in the background I could hear the clatter of mah-jongg tiles. There was a game going on, and he was probably eager to get back to it.

I spoke slowly in Chinese. "I want to know about a woman named Yee Winter-Flower."

"She's not here," the man said and hung up.

I called back immediately, but it took a dozen rings before the man answered this time, as if he was trying to ignore me. "Hello?"

I told myself to be patient. "I wasn't asking if the woman was there. I wanted to know if you could tell me about her."

"No," the man said and slammed the receiver down.

The third time it took twenty rings, and when the man picked up the phone, he snapped, "Go away."

If I was going to get an answer, I could see I was going to have to be persistent. "I will if you help me. She's the daughter of a friend that I'm trying to help."

"Do you know how many Yees there are?" the man asked, sounding harassed.

"Do you?" I challenged.

"No," he snapped. "But there are lots."

"This is important," I insisted.

The man swore under his breath and then said impatiently, "I'll check and call you." I could hear voices calling him back to the table. He warned the others not to peek at his hand. "What was that name again?"

I repeated the Chinese name: Yee Winter-Flower.

I gave him our number. I hoped he wasn't trying just to brush me off. "Please call."

"Yes, yes," he said and shouted another warning to his friends.

Then the line went dead. I tried to console myself with the fact that he had asked for the name of Wolf's daughter.

I changed into my sweats and went over to Leah's, working off Saturday's lunch in the practice room her father had built for her until I was ready to drop. When I got home, I was a little surprised when the man called back.

Perhaps he'd won some of the games, for he sounded almost cheerful. "Here is the information you requested," he said. "Try this number." And he rattled off a number as I struggled to find a pencil.

"Wait. She's dead," I said, but he had already hung up. I quickly wrote the number down and then stared at it. The area code didn't look familiar, so I assumed it was out of town.

I figured Mom would never notice a long-distance call if I kept it short. It would just get lost in the long list of other long-distance calls she made from home—helping Mad George's get off the ground was a twenty-four-hour job.

I set the phone on my lap and took a breath. Then I began to dial the number, listening to the phone sing to me as I poked its buttons. It rang about half a dozen times before a woman picked it up.

"What do you want?" a surly woman asked in Chinese.

"I'm an acquaintance of a man named Yee Golden-Promise," I began.

"Who?" the woman asked sharply.

I repeated the name. "I'm trying to find out about Yee Winter-Flower."

"Who's asking?" the woman said, suddenly suspicious.

"Me," I said.

"Did he put you up to this?" she demanded angrily.

Suddenly, I became wary. "Of course not."

"Who is this? Where are you?" The woman bristled with questions like a porcupine with sharp-pointed quills.

Something was wrong, but I didn't know what. "Sorry. I must have the wrong number," I said and slammed the phone down.

I figured the guy had given me any old number just to get me off his back, and then I had gotten some poor woman out of the bathtub. As far as I knew, it was a dead end.

That shows how much I knew.

FOURTEEN

Out of the Forest

The rest of the week, I tried to ignore what was happening in the family—Ian's sullen looks, the squabbling among my parents and my uncles. I tried to pretend I was living next to a construction site: There was a lot of ugly trash to see and a lot of loud noise to hear. You hate it, but you don't control it, so you just try to shut it out.

I narrowed my world down to two people, Grandmother and Wolf. During the week, I pumped Amy for more information and did research in the library. By Saturday, I was primed. When I got to the store after practice, sore and tired, I discovered that I wasn't the only one who had been preparing. Grandmother had gotten a new perm. And though her coat was buttoned up to the neck, I was sure she was wearing one of her fancy dresses underneath it.

My uncles were so absorbed in their feud that I

don't think they had even noticed the change in their mother. They were off in a corner, examining a thick stack of inventory sheets with Mom.

"Nice 'do," I said to Grandmother.

She patted it self-consciously to make sure it hadn't straightened out. "Do you really think so?"

Mom must have been keeping an eye out for me, though, because she crooked her finger at me. "Robin, can I talk to you?"

"Sure," I said.

"Don't tell her anything," Grandmother whispered.

I followed Mom into her office at the rear of the store. It was a narrow cubicle jammed with boxes of electrical equipment. In one corner was a metal desk heaped with invoices and her calculator. A tape with an unbroken flow of numbers in red ink on it ran from the desk onto the floor.

"What's going on?" Mom demanded.

I couldn't help thinking of Wolf. He would have wanted to know about my day, how ballet practice had gone, and all the other details of my life. He wouldn't have acted like a cop giving me the third degree.

Even if I hadn't promised Grandmother, I wouldn't have told Mom anything. "Nothing," I said.

Mom folded her arms. "You and Grandmother are up to something."

"Is she?" I asked, trying to sound innocent.

"She hasn't had her hair done since . . ." Mom's

eyebrows drew together as she tried to recall the day. "Well, since never."

"Maybe she wants to look nice." I shrugged.

Mom tapped her foot impatiently. "Why?"

"Why ask me? Why not ask her?" I said defensively.

Mom used a standard reply. "I'm asking you," she said primly.

I licked my lips. "Well, I don't know what your mother has in mind, but it wouldn't be bad or dangerous, would it?"

"Well, no," Mom admitted grudgingly.

"We just hang out," I said. That at least was true.

"Are you finished?" Grandmother said. She hovered in the doorway, leaning on her canes.

"Yes," I said, scurrying out to her before Mom could stop me.

"Good-bye," Grandmother said to Mom. "Don't worry. Robin will take good care of me."

"Thanks for rescuing me," I whispered to Grandmother as we made our escape.

"She was always nosy as a little girl," Grandmother said and jerked her head to the south. "Ah Wing will be waiting around the corner."

Sure enough, Ah Wing was there, lounging against his cab, his cap pushed back on his head. He was consulting a racing form.

"How did we do?" Grandmother asked.

"We didn't get it last week, but the pot's up to forty-eight million now," Ah Wing said, tucking his reading matter under his arm.

"All the more for us," Grandmother said cheerfully.

"Yeah, it'll be worth the wait," Ah Wing agreed.

I left the talking to Ah Wing and Grandmother while I thought over the things Amy had said. Dutiful. Quiet. Obedient.

When I saw the green-tiled roofs of Chinatown, I felt for the first time ever almost as if I was coming home.

Ah Wing dropped us off in front of the Celestial Forest and then went to park. Inside, we found Wolf in a newly pressed blue pinstriped suit, and his shoes looked freshly polished. He had had his hair cut. And when we got near him, I could smell his cologne.

The waiter complained to him. "You can't leave me like this." He waved a hand at the crowded restaurant.

"Ng can handle it." Wolf nodded in the direction of the kitchen.

"He's the dishwasher," the waiter scowled.

"I taught him a couple of things," Wolf said. "Just don't let them order anything but sweet-and-sour pork and wonton soup."

"They're the only good things here anyway," Ah Bock joked.

Wolf slapped him on the shoulder. "Pigs have a taste only for swill."

It sounded like a mean thing to say, but Ah Bock

didn't take any offense. In fact, he even chuckled at the insult as if he enjoyed the attention.

I remembered what Grandmother had said about Peter Pan and the Lost Boys. I plucked her coat sleeve, and she leaned close to me.

"Do you realize that if he's Peter Pan that makes you Wendy," I said.

"I can't ever talk to you seriously," she grumbled.

Wolf turned to us with a smile. "Would you like to see a movie?" He waved nervously at the room full of men. A lot of the faces looked familiar from last time. "I've asked all my friends with families what to do," he said. "Every father takes his family to a movie on the weekend. I thought we could do that before we had lunch."

I guess he'd done his homework, as I had.

I hesitated. The game was all well and good for the Celestial Forest, but should we really try to play it in the outside world?

I glanced uncertainly at Grandmother, noticing that she had dimples when she smiled.

"We'd love to," she said. "What are we going to see?"

"I don't know." Leaning toward me, Wolf smiled. "Is there anything you've been dying to go to?"

Despite all my preparation, the afternoon had veered off in a wildly different direction. I didn't have a clue what to do, and that made me feel totally help-less. "Not especially."

"I thought all girls had crushes on movie stars," he teased.

Now that he had decided I was too old for candy, he had substituted one set of stereotypes for another.

"Not at the moment," I said carefully.

He straightened. "Doesn't anyone want to see anything?" A little anxiety had crept into his voice.

"We're all being too polite," Grandmother said.

Ah Bock held up a folded newspaper, which Wolf took. "Let's look at the possibilities." Unfolding it, he held it out to me and Grandmother.

When I saw it was a Chinese paper, I really started to panic. I was blowing it again. "I can't read," I had to confess.

Wolf raised ink-smudged fingers to scratch his head. "You . . . can't?" he said, puzzled.

"I'm sorry," I said.

I hadn't realized how important these visits had become to Wolf. Fortunately he wanted to hold on to his fantasy. "We'll have to teach you," he chuckled. "You see, I'm not old-fashioned. I think girls should go to school."

"I'll take care of that," Grandmother promised.

I sighed with relief. Before I could make another mistake, I asked, "What's close? We shouldn't try to walk too far."

"Let's see," Wolf said, studying the newspaper. "What about a Jacky Chan movie? Everybody loves him. Have you seen *Young Master?*"

Grandmother's face lit up. "I love Jacky Chan."

"Who's Jacky Chan?" I asked Grandmother.

It was a turnabout of the usual situation in which Grandmother had to ask me about an American actor or singer. "He's a very good fighter," Grandmother explained.

"A kung fu movie?" I said, disappointed. Mom had taken me to a couple of them. They had been blood-fests with battles that dragged on forever.

"He's also very funny," Wolf added.

"Oh," I said doubtfully. I felt even less inclined to go. I had tried hard to understand Mom's Chinese humor. But whenever she told a joke in Chinese, I would wait and wait for the punch line long after everyone else had started to laugh.

"You don't want to go?" Wolf asked anxiously.

I reminded myself of Amy's advice. Dutiful, obedient.

"I'm looking forward to it," I said like a good Chinese daughter.

As we left, Ah Bock gave me a thumbs-up.

FIFTEEN

Young Master

Near Stockton Street stood a large movie theater. Looking at its rounded lines, I guessed it had been built in the fifties. The neon on the marquee sputtered and sizzled.

Wolf went up to the box office, where a middle-aged woman sat wearing a cardigan sweater. She was wearing black, heart-shaped glasses and she thumbed through a Chinese paperback.

"Two adults," Wolf began and then hesitated. "And one child."

The woman behind the counter studied me from different angles. "How old is she?"

"Twelve," Wolf said.

At the same time, looking up at the sign in Chinese and English, I said, "Eleven." That was the maximum age for a child's admission.

"Which is it?" the woman demanded.

"Well, I . . ." Wolf glanced at me uncertainly.

Fortunately, Grandmother stepped in. "She's twelve in Chinese years, eleven in American." And she explained to me, "The Chinese count the time in the womb as the first year of life."

The woman rose up from her seat to eye me suspiciously. "She's too tall for eleven. She has to be older. Do you have any identification with your picture on it? Maybe a student I.D.?"

Before I could hunt for my wallet, Wolf took charge. "She left it at home," he said hastily. "So give me another adult."

"Three adults," the woman said triumphantly. The springs squeaked as she plopped back down on her seat and tore the tickets.

Wolf pulled crumpled dollar bills out of his pocket, smoothing them on the little sill in front of the window opening. I wondered if they represented his share of the day's tips and how many plates of chow mein it had taken to earn them.

Grandmother felt bad, too. "So expensive," she murmured.

"You're my one luxury," Wolf smiled, picking up the tickets and leading us inside.

The theater's lobby had a floor of ugly brick-red concrete, and the glossy white paint on the walls was beginning to peel. And yet through all the layers of paint, I could see some of the original plaster ornamentation: urns decorated with bulls, and growing from the urns, tall vines that spread up the walls and over the ceiling. It must have been a stage theater at one time—with the front modernized later.

To our left were the doors to the restrooms and to our right was a snack counter.

"How about some treats?" Wolf asked us.

I'd been counting on lunch, so I was grateful at the prospect of some popcorn. "No butter, please."

He laughed. "Butter? Whatever for?"

Wolf led us to the snack counter. Through the glass, I saw rows of Chinese candies and preserved fruit. The soda machine itself was empty and its dusty glass sides suggested it hadn't been used in a long time. Instead, there were stacks of various soy drinks in cardboard boxes next to it. Wolf bought us some salted watermelon seeds. "These won't make you fat."

I stared at the seeds. They had a reddish tinge as if they had been dyed. I didn't have the faintest notion how to eat them.

"Thank you," I said as I took my packet of seeds. I stuffed them into a pocket, intending to forget them there.

"Ooo, I love these," Grandmother said as she took hers.

Wolf beamed. "So do I."

When I pushed open the swinging door into the theater, I saw that the movie had already started. Even with the film flashing on the big rectangular screen, it seemed pitch-black inside. "The theater's dark. We should see if there's an usher with a flashlight."

"No need." Wolf produced a flashlight out of his pocket. "I expected this, too."

Grandmother patted his arm gratefully. "You've thought of everything."

"I've tried to," he smiled shyly. "There's too much that can go wrong in life."

I wondered how long he had been planning this afternoon. Perhaps the whole week?

The flashlight cast an oval of light that swayed this way and that as we headed inside. The floor inside the theater matched the red floor of the lobby. Grandmother took my arm while Wolf led us down the aisle.

Even though the actors' voices boomed from the speakers, there seemed to be even more noise inside the theater. Half a dozen people were carrying on conversations in regular voices, and little cracking noises followed by tiny *whooshes* occurred all over the theater.

"Here're three," Wolf said, shining his light on three seats, and we slid into them.

Grandmother nudged me excitedly. "That's Jacky Chan," she said, pointing to a young man with long hair who had appeared on the screen. He was of medium height with a solid build and was as supple as a rubber snake.

"The subtitles are in Chinese," I whispered.

Grandmother answered in her normal voice, just as the other customers were doing. "The actors are speaking Cantonese, so the producers have to put the Chinese characters in the subtitles. That way speakers of other dialects can understand. Especially the ones who use Mandarin." Most Chinese speak Mandarin.

"I'll explain to you," Wolf said from my other side. Then I heard a sharp little *crack* and small *whoosh* from his seat. It took a moment for me to realize that he was cracking open a watermelon seed and then spitting the shell on the floor. From around the theater, I heard half a dozen people making the same sounds. And then Grandmother started to snack on the seeds, too.

My feet made crackling noises from the old, discarded shells on the concrete. Slowly I raised them and propped them on the back of the seat in front of me.

Soon I got lost in the movie as some villains caught Jacky Chan while he was disguised as a woman. For the first time, people in the theater stopped talking.

"Remember when my crazy uncle got drunk?" Wolf said to Grandmother. "He tried to put on his wife's good dress and tore every seam. Was she ever mad."

"Oh, yes," Grandmother said, laughing.

It was hard both to listen to them and watch the movie, but I tried. The scene was really funny because Jacky Chan's dress kept him from kicking very high. "What's he saying now?" I asked Wolf.

Wolf was only too happy to translate the subtitles for me. And with the help of his commentary, I could follow the story. Jacky Chan played a servant who had followed his disgraced master into exile, but then had gotten separated from him. And Jacky Chan was as funny as some of the best silent screen comedians—like Charlie Chaplin. It was possible to be graceful, athletic, and yet comic.

Every now and then Wolf would point to something else that reminded him of his home in China and reminisce with Grandmother. Now this was what I had been studying for the entire week. I got ready to leap in as the ideal daughter, but they talked about many different things back in China—names, phrases, song titles—that they didn't bother to explain to me.

Of course, the movie ended happily. Jacky helped restore his master's reputation, and they returned home in honor.

When the lights went up, Grandmother sighed. "That was marvelous."

Wolf brushed spare bits of shell from his shirt. "Did you enjoy it?" he asked me.

"It was a lot of fun," I said, swinging my feet back down to the shell-covered floor.

"I have something else," Wolf said. He put his hand in a jacket pocket, but he was so nervous he got all tangled up. It took a couple of tugs before he freed a red silk pouch and held it out to Grandmother.

Grandmother just stared at the dangling pouch. "What is it?"

"Open it," he urged her.

Reluctantly she took it and opened the drawstrings. With trembling fingers, she lifted out a pair of jade earrings with gold pins. "What?"

Wolf squirmed with happiness. "I remembered you wanted them as a girl."

Grandmother tried to hand both pouch and earrings back to him. "I can't take them."

Wolf sat back hurt. "Do you already have a pair?"

"It's one thing to treat us to lunch or a movie, but this . . ." Grandmother shook her head and handed them back.

Wolf's frustration increased the more she refused until finally he turned to me. Taking my hand, he turned it palm upward and slapped the purse and earrings onto it. "Here, you take them."

Suddenly, I began to realize why Grandmother didn't want to take them. To do that would be stepping over some new boundary—one more daring and demanding than stepping outside the Celestial Forest.

"I can't," I said.

"Don't be like your . . . your mother," Wolf grumbled.

I felt caught between the two of them. I glanced helplessly at Grandmother, who shrugged. "Oh, take them."

Wolf tried to get us to have lunch next, but Grand-mother had suddenly lost her appetite. We had to go back to the restaurant anyway to get Ah Wing, and no one seemed particularly happy with the way the after-noon had ended.

As Ah Wing sped out of Chinatown, Grandmother said, "Let us pay you this time. We don't have any food." It would have to be out of our pocket, too. This time the waiter hadn't slipped us any money.

Ah Wing dismissed the suggestion with a wave of his hand. "It's for Wolf."

"I think Wolf likes you," I said to Grandmother.

"I wish I knew why," she said doubtfully.

"Well," I said, considering my words carefully, "you're smart. You're pretty."

She hung her head like a frightened little girl. "No."

"Yes."

Grandmother continued to stare at her booted feet, so I put my arm around her shoulders. "Really," I said.

She just shook her head and spoke in a low voice so Ah Wing couldn't hear. "My mother told me I was as ugly as a water buffalo. The only thing that would make me pretty was binding my feet."

I had once seen Grandmother's feet. The toes had been bent under the soles. Even though she didn't bind her feet anymore, they were still crippled. Some days every step caused her pain. Whenever my own dancing injuries hurt a little, I reminded myself that

Grandmother went through pain a thousand times worse.

I rested my cheek against hers. "I don't understand how anyone could do that to a little girl," I whispered back.

Grandmother raised a hand and stroked my hair. "In the old days, it was the thing to do. That's why my mother beat me when I cried from the pain. She said I was being stupid and ungrateful. So I learned long ago to keep everything inside."

And never let anyone know they had hurt her. That helped explain why she clammed up so much about her secrets and kept them all tucked away inside her heart. "Like tears?" I asked.

"And thoughts and memories," Grandmother admitted ruefully and then added, "and feelings."

"I'm sorry, Grandmother," I said, hugging her again. "I won't ever hurt you. And you know Wolf now. He wouldn't either."

She looked at her boots as if she could see her crippled feet through the leather. "Do you think . . . Wolf thinks I'm pretty because of my feet? Men do, you know. My husband did."

It was a strange notion of beauty, but millions of girls had once had their feet bound. So there must have been plenty of people at the time who thought such crippling was lovely.

For a moment, Grandmother seemed not like my

strong grandmother but like the little girl she had been. Scared. Alone. Hurting.

I hugged her tight. "They love you because you're you—just like I do."

Ah Wing, who'd been trying to eavesdrop, demanded in frustration, "Speak up, will you? What's wrong? Why didn't you stay for lunch?"

"None of your business," Grandmother snapped in her normal tone.

Ah Wing had been making his own guesses though. "He likes you, you know."

Grandmother seemed to huddle in herself. "Maybe, but this sort of thing is for someone like Robin, who's young."

"Didn't you hear?" Ah Wing asked. "When you come to America, they roll back the clock. You can be whatever age you feel."

"I'm not about to change," Grandmother grumbled.

"You're over here now, not back home," Ah Wing scolded her gently. "Things are different here. People become different, too."

"Not me," Grandmother insisted stubbornly.

"You're a fine-looking woman," Ah Wing said, pounding the steering wheel. "It'd be a crime to hide away."

Grandmother was quiet the rest of the way to her apartment. "Would you rather not go next Saturday?" I asked.

"Yes—no—I don't know," she said frantically. She paused thoughtfully for a moment and then added, "If I do end it, I should tell him to his face." She clutched at my arm. "But you have to go, too."

I remembered the movie theater. "Wouldn't I be in the way?" I asked.

Her fingers squeezed tighter. "I need you for support. I won't go without you."

"Then I'll be there," I promised.

SIXTEEN

To Grandmother's House

Because of her children's curiosity, Grandmother had asked me to meet her at her apartment after practice that Saturday. When I got there, Ah Wing was already parked outside. "You're late," he said, holding up his wrist so I could see the time on his watch.

"Sorry," I said. Though it hurt my toes, I ran the last few strides to Grandmother's.

The moment I buzzed at her doorbell, she jerked the door open.

"It's about time," she snapped.

She was already in her red cloth coat like last time, and her big black bag was in her hand. She'd even put on lipstick and makeup for the occasion, and her perm, because it was breezy outside, was protected by a scarf.

"I'm sorry, Grandmother. Practice ran late." I dumped my bag in a corner. "What are you going to say to him?"

Grandmother studied her reflection in the mirror

and adjusted the knot of her scarf. "I expect to say 'Hello.' "

I nudged her in the ribs. "You know."

She turned with a twinkle in her eye. "Know what?"

"Quit teasing me," I growled through gritted teeth.

She turned back to study her image. "I don't suppose it would do any harm to see each other," she said shyly.

"That's wonderful," I said, hugging her impulsively.

Grandmother pushed me away. "Now don't get carried away. We might not make it past the next movie."

When we stepped out onto the sidewalk, Ah Wing opened a creaky car door. "Your magic chariot awaits," he announced grandly. Once we were inside, he ran around the cab and got behind the wheel.

Ah Wing pulled an imaginary cord. "Next stop, Chinatown."

We shot like a rocket across town. You couldn't have told from Grandmother's expression that she was excited, but she didn't want to talk much.

When we got to the Celestial Forest, there was a crowd outside on the sidewalk. Tourists and old-timers brushed shoulders as they tried to steal a peek inside the restaurant.

"Oh, no," Grandmother muttered, peering through the window, "poor Wolf."

Fearing the worst, we got out of Ah Wing's double-parked taxi and squeezed between two parked cars and onto the sidewalk. Once we were there, I used my elbows and hips to wriggle through the crowd. Fortunately, I'd been well trained by Grandmother at the Richmond fruit stands and garage sales. All the time that I bumped and elbowed, I kept muttering, "Excuse me," in both Chinese and English. Behind me, I could hear Grandmother doing the same.

When I got near the window, I peered through the dusty glass. The restaurant was deserted inside, but the tables and chairs were overturned—looking like strange, dead beasts with their feet sticking up into the air.

The waiter was sitting on the floor with a napkin dispenser on his lap and a napkin pressed against his mouth. As I watched, he lowered the napkin and studied the blood on it. Then he tossed it on a little pile of discards, pulled a new napkin from the dispenser, and held that one against his mouth.

"The waiter's bleeding," I said to Grandmother over my shoulder. The mob was particularly thick around the door. "Let me through." I don't remember whether I used English or Chinese as I fought my way through them. Behind me, I could hear an occasional "ow" as if Grandmother were now poking people with her canes.

Blocking the doorway itself was a particularly big man in a blue windbreaker. He had his camcorder pressed up against his eye and was videotaping everything from the waiter to the ceiling—even the god of war. He reminded me of some kind of vulture.

"Coming through," I said. I hadn't gone shopping with Grandmother for nothing. Jamming my heel down hard on the man's toes, I hit him with my elbow at the same time.

"Hey," he protested as he fell backward among the other spectators.

Once I had scooted through the space he left into the restaurant itself, I turned to help Grandmother. But she squirted through the hole in the crowd as if she were greased.

Once we were inside, we could hear loud shouting coming from within the kitchen. It sounded like two people. One voice was Wolf's and the other a woman's.

The waiter turned to me as he disposed of another bloody napkin. I could see that his lip was split. "You'd better go," he said.

"What's happened to Wolf?" Grandmother started to cross the restaurant, but it was easy to race around her.

The waiter lunged as I passed, trying to grab me, but I managed to get around him. "It's a disaster. He doesn't need you now."

I'm the kind of person who always covers her eyes when the scary part of a horror film comes on—but I always wind up peeking through my fingers. So I couldn't resist going to see what was happening in the kitchen.

I got to the kitchen doorway just in time to see the

dishwasher running toward me in the same stained apron he had worn last week.

"Duck," he said.

It's a good thing I crouched when he did, because a big bowl of uncooked wonton smashed against the wall.

"Grandmother, are you okay?" I asked, looking behind me.

She was picking off wonton that had fallen on her during the bowl's flight. "Where's Wolf?"

It was the woman who threw it. I thought it would have taken someone as strong as a weight-lifter to toss something as heavy as that, but she was a skinny thing. She looked as if she was in her forties, and her short hair stuck up in places as if she didn't comb it. Though she wore a drab gray polyester suit, underneath it was a bright orange-and-yellow blouse.

Wolf was standing, arguing with her. Bits of food covered his face and clothes, so I assumed that some of her tosses had found their mark. He seemed to be pleading while the woman scolded him. They were both speaking Chinese too fast for me to follow.

"Leave him alone," I said in Chinese to the woman.

I tried to step in front of Wolf to shield him, but he tried to shove me away. "No, no, I deserve this," he insisted humbly.

"Deserve? Deserve?" the woman screeched. I only understood about a third of what she said. "You dirty———. I ought to———. Filthy———." Reaching for the nearest object, she tried to lift a pot by its handles.

They were hot, so she let it go, wringing her hands in pain. But she had just managed to tip the pot over.

"Watch out, that's boiling stock!" Wolf said.

Shoving me aside with one hand, he grabbed the woman with the other and yanked her away as hot soup splashed over the floor.

"My feet," the woman moaned. Putting a hand up to her face, she began to cry.

"Let's go," I told Wolf, thinking it was a good time to make our escape.

And in the doorway Grandmother was motioning to him. "This way."

However, to our amazement, he walked over to the woman and put his arms around her. "There, there," he said, patting her on the back.

After a little while, her weeping subsided. He led her out of the kitchen and we followed. "Let's check for burns," he said gently.

"It's all your fault," she hiccuped.

Wolf seated the woman on the nearest chair. Then, getting onto one knee with difficulty, he began to untie her shoe. "How many times have I told you not to come into a kitchen where things are boiling and frying?" He spoke gently, like a parent to a child.

"If the kitchen's such a dangerous place, you should have made me leave," she said, frowning.

I rolled my eyes at that, but Wolf kindly took the

blame. "It's all my fault. I'm sorry," he said, yanking off the shoe.

I saw plenty of bunions, but no burn marks.

She wriggled her toes as she studied them. "I bet the shoe is ruined."

Wolf switched to the other foot. "How's your other one?"

"Wet," she said sullenly.

"But it doesn't hurt?" he asked.

"No."

He checked anyway, and then went into the kitchen. The woman and I stared at each other. "What are you gawking at?" she demanded.

"N-nothing," I stuttered.

"Well, go look at some other nothing," she said. She had been holding her feet suspended in the air but now rested them on the bottom rung of the chair, where she perched like some large, bad-tempered owl.

"Come on, you two." It was the waiter, his voice muffled by the napkin. "This time, listen to me." He gripped my shoulder and began to draw me back toward the front door.

"What's going on?" Grandmother asked, standing her ground.

"So I got you," the woman laughed harshly at the waiter. "Serves you right." There was gloating in her voice.

Wolf came out of the kitchen with an old towel. "Let me dry your feet."

The woman didn't move her feet from the rung that joined the chair's legs. "The towel's dirty."

"No, it's clean. Just old." Wolf held it up in his hands so she could inspect it.

"Break it up, folks. Break it up." A tall policeman shouldered his way through the crowd and into the restaurant.

He tilted his hat back as he took in the wreckage. "So what's happened here? A gang fight?"

"No, no, just a little misunderstanding," the waiter said hastily.

The policeman pushed aside the waiter's hand that held the napkin to his lip. "You're going to need stitches for that cut. I'd call that more than a misunderstanding."

Wolf stood up, leaving the towel with the woman. "He and I were having a fight," he said, nodding to the waiter.

Grandmother looked as if she was going to protest, but Wolf gave her a little shake of his head.

The policeman took out a notebook. "Name?"

The waiter gave his. "Ah Sam."

"Address?"

The waiter gave a number that must have been a room up above the restaurant.

When the policeman aimed his pen at Wolf, Wolf said, "Yee Golden-Promise." He lived upstairs as well.

The policeman turned to Grandmother then. "Yours?"

"She wasn't here for the fight," Wolf tried to explain.

The policeman wagged his pen at him. "I won't warn you again to be quiet."

Grandmother provided her name and address and tried to head off trouble by introducing me. "And that's my granddaughter, Robin," she said and then gave my address.

"And yours?" the policeman called to the woman.

She was still wiping her feet. "What does that ox want?" she asked in Chinese.

"Your name and address," the waiter said.

"Yee Winter-Flower." She had an address that was down in San Diego.

"Another Yee, huh?" the policeman said and pointed his pen back and forth between Wolf and the woman. "Any relation?"

Wolf swallowed. "She's my daughter."

"But I thought she starved to death," I said in Chinese to the waiter.

"So did we at one time," the waiter replied.

"But why—" I began.

He wouldn't look us in the eye. "Don't talk about her right now. Your Grandmother understands."

Next to me, Grandmother nodded her head dazedly. "Is . . . is there a wife too?"

"No," the waiter said. "She's definitely dead."

I took Grandmother's hand and gave it a sympathetic squeeze. Even if the wife was dead, the presence of the daughter changed everything now. And just when Grandmother had been willing to open herself up to a new relationship. It didn't seem fair.

The cop stared at me curiously the way people always did when I spoke Chinese. "Hey, speak only English."

I helped Grandmother sit down on a chair, and then I needed to plop down myself. I felt as if I'd just been hit by a frying pan. Could this sloppy, vulgar woman be Wolf's real daughter? I kept stealing peeks at her. She seemed indifferent to the whole world as she dried out her shoes.

In the meantime, Wolf and the waiter had been making up a pretty good-sounding explanation of a fight for the sake of the policeman. While the cop was interrogating the waiter, Wolf looked over at us, pleading with his eyes for us to stay quiet.

After the policeman had taken down Wolf's statement, he called to Wolf's real daughter. "Is that how it happened?"

The daughter looked not at him but at Wolf.

"Tell him yes," Wolf said.

"Yes," the woman said, imitating the English syllable with difficulty.

"I'll need to see some identification from each of you," the policeman said.

"Certainly," Wolf said, reaching into his back

pocket. At the same time, the waiter took a driver's license from his wallet.

The policeman barely glanced at them and then jerked his head at Winter-Flower. "And yours?"

Winter-Flower jammed her feet unconcernedly into her shoes. "What did he say, white girl?"

When I told her, she drew her arms in against her sides as if she were shrinking. "I'm not going back to China."

"Please, she's innocent," Wolf said to the policeman.

The policeman busily waved Wolf to be quiet as he turned to me. "What did she say?"

Before I could answer, Winter-Flower shouted in Chinese, "I'm not going back." She shot up from the chair so fast that her head hit the policeman's jaw, knocking him backward. Stepping over him, she bolted for the door. I thought she'd smack against the crowd there, but she was so skinny she wiggled right into it and disappeared.

"Come back here!" the cop said, but even though he was big and strong, he could make it only as far as the threshold because of the crowd.

The waiter darted over to the cash register and punched at the keys. The drawer shot out with a musical clink. "Quick. Find her and get out of the city." He pulled up handfuls of paper money.

"Thank you," Wolf said, stuffing the bundle into his pants.

He turned to Grandmother. "I'm sorry. For a while, you made me young again. But even if I have to grow old again, you keep on staying young. One door closes but another one opens."

"What are you going to do?" I asked.

"What I should have done long ago. Be with my daughter." Wolf smiled at me. "My younger daughter makes me very happy and very proud, too."

I was so choked up that it took me a moment to say, "Don't go."

He was already heading for the kitchen. "Thank you," he said in English to me and Grandmother. And then he disappeared inside. In a moment, I heard the back door slam, and Wolf had vanished.

SEVENTEEN

Wolf's Cub

"What's going on? Why was she so scared of the police?" I asked the waiter.

He slowly slid the drawer shut. "I'll explain in a moment."

Outside we could see the head of the policeman above the crowd. The people near him were trying to obey and back away, but the rest of the crowd held them in place.

I put my hand under the waiter's elbow to support him. "Are you all right?"

He tried to smile but winced at the pain. "I have a nephew who's a doctor. I'll go see him in a minute." He caught sight of the dishwasher, who was getting to his feet. "You. Straighten up the tables and chairs."

The dishwasher began to restore the restaurant at a snail's pace. The waiter gazed at him in disgust.

"Was that awful woman really his daughter?"

Wolf's daughter had been such a pleasant fantasy. I had invented a sweet, creative girl. It was hard to reconcile my dream with that angry person who had been shouting and throwing dishes.

"You heard Wolf," the waiter said, as if he was still trying to protect his friend.

"You owe us an explanation," Grandmother said, her voice shaking. "You used us."

His head dipped. "I paid you."

I slammed a hand against the chair back. "Do you think we did it for your money?"

His lip still bleeding, the waiter sat down suddenly as if he was feeling weak—perhaps from loss of blood. "She disappeared when the Japanese invaded China. He thought she was dead but she was waiting for him to come for her. Then she wound up in Fukien."

My geography was pretty sketchy. "Where's that?" I asked, getting a chair for Grandmother.

"It's a province on the ocean, but above Kwang-tung," she explained sullenly.

That helped explain the woman's anger. A lot of resentment could build up over the years while you waited for your father to come.

The waiter fumbled at the table's napkin dispenser. "She saved up her money to come over here."

"She came here to find him," Grandmother nodded.

The waiter frowned. "She traveled on one of those boats. Packed in with hardly any air or food or water."

When he saw my puzzled look, he spoke more plainly. "She came here illegally. She landed in San Diego a few years ago. Since then she's been down there working off her passage."

I supposed I ought to give her points for that. "But then why was she screaming at him?"

The waiter started to shake his head. "When the cook heard she was here, he went down to visit her. She wanted him to pay off her passage money. But he's as poor as she is. When he couldn't, she got angry."

Grandmother nodded. "It must have been a big disappointment for her. She couldn't have had it easy in China. She would have built up big dreams about her father."

The waiter closed his eyes. "And then, after she got here on her own, he couldn't do a thing to help her."

"So she got mad," Grandmother said.

He opened his eyes and blinked them several times as he tried to focus again. "You saw what a temper she has. She got so angry that she disowned him. They haven't spoken since."

Grandmother nodded slowly. "So the cook was depressed over the breakup."

"You told us she starved to death," I accused the waiter.

The waiter's breath made the bottom edge of the napkin pressed against his lip flutter as he talked. "I told you what we thought had happened. I didn't know you that well. For all I knew, you might have told the wrong people and gotten her in trouble. The immigration service has spies everywhere."

"If someone's here illegally, you shouldn't talk about it to anyone," Grandmother explained.

I was feeling a little dizzy myself, so I sat down. "So why did she show up today?"

"I don't know." The napkin tore in his hand, leaving a small white patch still clinging to his lower lip. A small red dot on the patch of napkin slowly widened. "She came in, shouting that someone had called up the Yee family association. They were looking for Wolf's family. She figured it was some social worker trying to rope her into helping her father because he was sick."

That must have been my phone call. "So she came up here to find him?" I asked hopefully.

"Yes. She was so upset that she borrowed money for the bus ticket and went into even more debt." The waiter took another napkin from the dispenser. "Just so she could tell him to leave her alone. She said he had no claim on her now."

I wrinkled my forehead. "That doesn't sound very Chinese." My own mother had sacrificed almost everything to bring Grandmother over from Hong Kong.

"Maybe China was never the way we imagined it," he sighed.

I braced myself against the back of the chair. "But Wolf wasn't looking to her for support."

The small red dot continued to widen. "Ever try to explain something to a firecracker when it's busy exploding?" Because of his cut lip, the waiter didn't try to smile, but he did laugh. "He was better off with a part-time daughter like you."

When we heard footsteps, the waiter turned to the door. "We're not open yet," he said in Chinese.

A family of tourists hesitated by the door, staring at the restaurant, which was only half restored. They were wearing sweatshirts with different San Francisco landmarks on them and shorts. "You got a menu?"

The crowd had dispersed once the fighting was over. No one wanted to watch a waiter sit and talk—even if his lip was split. And a new bunch of tourists had wandered in.

The waiter stared at the family a moment. "Wait," he said in English. Throwing away the napkin, he pointed at the dishwasher. "Hey, you, Ng," he said in Chinese.

The dishwasher straightened with a chair clutched in his hands. "What's wrong now?"

The waiter went over to Ng and yanked the chair from his hands. "You've just been promoted to cook. Don't worry. I won't let any of them order anything too fancy." As Ng shambled slowly toward the kitchen, the waiter planted the chair firmly at a big circular table. "Please, sit down," he urged the tourist family in English.

I almost warned them, but Grandmother gave her

head a little shake. I suppose it was a compliment, in a way, that the waiter was asking us to keep his secret.

The waiter busied himself with getting menus and cans of American soda for them. Funny, but before I met Grandmother, I wouldn't have found it strange to drink American sodas with a Chinese meal. However, after many meals with Grandmother, I knew there were all sorts of nice teas. Maybe I was starting to fit in a little after all.

When the waiter had got the tourists settled, another family came in. "Sit down," he said, waving them over to another big circular table.

Then he went back to the first table, where he kept his word to the dishwasher. "No, no—no egg rolls today."

The father started to point to another part of the menu. "Well, what about—"

"No, no—no mu shu pork," the waiter said firmly.

They went through half a dozen dishes before the father finally said in exasperation, "Well, what do you have?"

The waiter shifted from one foot to the other and then announced, "Sweet-and-sour pork and wonton soup."

"For six?" the mother asked skeptically.

"I'm hungry," the littlest one said.

The father motioned resignedly with his menu at the child. "You want to find another place?"

"Well," the mother hesitated, glancing at the littlest. She seemed to be weighing satisfying her stomach against the possibility of a tantrum.

"I speak American," the waiter declared proudly. "Maybe at the next place they don't."

That was the deciding factor. With a large sigh, the mother held out her menu as a token of her surrender. The waiter gathered up all the menus like giant cards and went on to the next table where he repeated his performance until he had an additional five orders for sweet-and-sour pork.

He was rather pleased with himself by the time he came back to us. "So the afternoon won't be a total loss," he said in Chinese. Out of habit, he selected a couple of menus from his armful and started to hand them to us. "Would you like to order anything? I know you must be hungry." He stopped when he remembered who was cooking. "Just be sure you want only sweet-and-sour pork and wonton soup."

I thought of the dishwasher and lost any appetite I'd had. "No thanks."

While she had been waiting, Grandmother had been squirming worriedly in her chair. "How did Wolf react when he saw his daughter for the first time?" she finally got to ask the waiter.

I could only guess what she was feeling at the moment. I felt sorry for her.

The waiter fanned the menus out like a hand of

cards. "Pretty good, considering she was trying to brain him with a pot."

"It's all my fault," I said, feeling guilty.

Grandmother drew her eyebrows together in puzzlement. "You didn't do anything."

Even the waiter tried to assure me. "It was fate."

"No, I started it." I felt their eyes studying me alertly as I confessed. "I was the one who called the family association. I started the whole thing."

"Why?" Grandmother demanded sharply.

"I'm so sorry. I was trying to do research." When they both looked puzzled, I went on. "So I . . . I could be a better daughter."

I felt helpless at that moment. I didn't know how to tell them it had been so nice to be part of a happy family—no matter how temporary. And also part of something even bigger. "I felt Chinese."

Grandmother sat back as if surprised. "You are Chinese," she insisted.

I gave her a hug. "I guess I am when I'm around you."

Grandmother patted me reassuringly. "It's inside you."

"You have to be Chinese, or you couldn't have made him happy. He stopped drinking after he met you," the waiter said.

"So we made him happy?" Grandmother asked. If we had made Wolf happy, he had made her the same— even if only for a little while.

The waiter hesitated and then nodded. "Very."

I felt a warm glow at that. Then some good had come of our fantasy. I turned and looked at the street.

I hoped Wolf and his real daughter could talk and work things out. I hoped for a lot of things as I stared out the window.

EIGHTEEN

Wolf's Song

The next morning, I still felt miserable about spoiling things for Grandmother. We had waited for a while in the restaurant, but when Ah Wing didn't show up, we had the waiter call us a taxi. Grandmother had said nothing to me on the way home.

As I lay there in bed feeling awful, I remembered what Wolf had said as he left: One door closes but another one opens.

So what do you do when you break something beautiful? You pick up the pieces and get on with your life. I might have lost my fantasy family, but I still had my original one—sort of.

Television makes you think that all families are automatically happy, but now I realized they are not. We were all going to have to work at being a real family as much as Grandmother and Wolf and I had worked at being a fantasy one.

Someone had to get the ball started rolling, though. So with the seeds of a plan beginning to sprout in my head, I went downstairs to the street and brought up the fat Sunday newspaper, but instead of reading the comics, I got everything ready for breakfast—the pancake batter mixed up, the butter and syrup out on the table with the plates and silverware.

"Hello." Dad yawned as he shuffled into the kitchen.

I pulled out a chair. "Coffee's all ready."

"I know. I could smell it." He plopped down in a chair.

"And here's the paper." I set it down before him and then turned to pour him a cup of coffee. When I brought it to him, he was staring at the untouched newspaper.

He smiled timidly. "I can't remember the last time I had a whole newspaper to read." He flapped a hand to his left and right. "Usually Mom gets to the newspaper first and scatters the sections all around."

I set the cup down. "I can mess it up for you."

He slapped his hands protectively over the newspaper. "Not a chance."

He made a point of starting to read the comics then, so I busied myself making pancakes. There are all kinds of household silences. There's the calm before the storm, and there's the happy quiet when everyone goes about his routine. It's warm enough to wrap around yourself like a blanket. And then there's the kind when everyone is aching inside because something is wrong and talking only makes the hurt deeper and sharper. And that was the kind of silence in our kitchen.

Still, I tried to carry on. "Breakfast," I said.

"Oh, boy," he said, clapping his hands together and rubbing his palms as if eager for food.

I noticed that he was still reading the first page of the comics, but I didn't say anything as I shoveled pancakes onto his plate. "Say when." At four, I stopped.

"I didn't say when," he teased.

"I heard your conscience pleading with me. He and I have our own private hook-up." I put one pancake on my plate but decided to treat myself to plenty of syrup.

From long habit, I cut my portion into small pieces and took my time chewing each one. As a result, I ate half of my pancake while Dad polished off two of his.

He was starting on the next two when Mom came in. She was wearing a pink, padded silk bathrobe. "Robin made us pancakes," Dad told her with a nervous smile.

Mom looked really bad, as if she hadn't slept all night. "I need my coffee first," she said, blinking wearily.

Dad looked concerned and started to say something but then shut his mouth and cleared his throat instead as he rattled the papers.

"I'll get it for you," I said, rising with my plate.

"No, don't bother." Mom got a cup from the cabinet and then slid the pot from the coffeemaker and poured herself a cup. "I've got to be at the store in an hour."

I put my plate in the sink and got milk from the fridge. "Milk?"

Mom smiled. "Thank you." She bit her lip as she carefully poured the milk into her coffee. When she took a sip, her shoulders relaxed and she smiled blissfully. "Ah, just the right temperature."

As she sat down, Dad companionably shoved the newspaper toward her. "What section would you like?"

Mom flipped through the sections and then glanced at the one Dad had in his hand. "That one."

With a loud sigh, Dad passed it on to her. "You haven't changed." And then he turned to me to explain. "Your mother did this on the first day we were married."

"Can I help if you have good taste?" Mom teased. "But this is nice." She refolded the sections until they were neat again and began to read. Instead of finding another section, Dad watched her with a fascinated smile—almost as if she were some rare bird that had settled at our kitchen table.

By her fourth sip of coffee, Mom had mellowed considerably. "Those pancakes do smell good."

"I'm hungry." Ian stumbled sleepily into the kitchen, rubbing his eyes.

"I'll make you some breakfast," I laughed. I was the cook's daughter, after all.

While I began to beat up the batter again, Ian went through the newspaper until he found the comics. He immediately thrust them between Dad and the sports pages. "Will you read them to me?" When Dad began to read *Dagwood*, Mom put down her paper, and Ian snuggled onto Dad's lap.

By the time Dad finished the comic section, the pancakes were ready. I'd made Ian one with Mickey Mouse ears. As he drowned Mickey in syrup, he looked around the table. "I wish we could stay like this always."

"It would be nice." Dad paused and then suggested wistfully, "I could call in sick."

"I'd love to do the same," Mom said, looking guilty. "But what about Eddy and Georgie?"

I thought of Wolf and his daughter. "Maybe there have been enough wrongs done in the name of family," I said.

With a moan, Mom put her elbows on the table and cradled her head in her hands. "I don't know what I'm supposed to do."

Dad patted her back sympathetically. "Maybe we ought to end the bickering. You know, like we talked about."

"You mean separate?" Mom asked, shocked.

I jumped up. This cure was even worse than the disease. "No, I'll be good. I promise," I said frantically.

"So will I," Ian said, just as desperately.

Mom reached forward and took my hand and then Ian's. "Whatever happens, it's neither of your faults."

Dad scratched his nose. "All I was trying to suggest was counseling."

Mom looked relieved. I think the specter of splitting up had shaken her as much as it had Ian and me. "A neutral referee might be good."

It was the first time in several weeks that they had agreed on anything.

"We should get somebody who understands multicultural marriages," Dad suggested.

"I know just the counselor," Mom nodded. "My friend Clare went to her."

Dad rubbed his temple. "The one who watched wrestling all the time?"

"That's her," Mom said. "Her husband collected bugs."

"You and I aren't nearly as bad," Dad said.

Mom gave him a thumbs-up. "Piece of cake."

Dad folded his arms. "The question is when."

Mom shrugged. "We'll have to make time."

Dad sighed. "I can adjust my schedule, but can you?"

Between her two jobs, Mom was gone fourteen to sixteen hours a day. She massaged her forehead. "I guess I'll have to, somehow."

Dad put his around her. "You know one of the first questions the counselor will ask is: Do you want to be part of your family business?"

Mom squirmed. "Eddy and Georgie need help so bad."

"This isn't about being Chinese or American," Dad said, keeping his gaze steady on Mom. "This is about being yourself."

"Well, I . . ." Mom stopped and then inclined her head. "Well, no. My regular job already takes up enough time." Mom looked surprised when she admitted that. I don't think she had let herself think about such things while she tried to meet her family obligations.

Ian snapped his fingers. "I bet Grandmother would help you get some time off."

"Just an hour a week for the counselor," Dad said.

Mom knew her brothers' precarious finances better than anyone. "There's no money to hire a temp to replace me," Mom said.

"Not even to help us work things out?" Dad asked, puzzled.

Mom shook her head. "My mother would never go for it. She always told me the family comes first."

"Well, we're your family, too," Dad pointed out.

Mom sat silent for a moment and then spoke slowly, more to herself than to us. "I guess you are."

Ian wrinkled his forehead. "Why are you guessing what Grandmother would say. Why not ask her?"

Mom's shoulders slumped. "It'd just be a waste of time."

"If you don't ask, you don't find out," Dad said.

"Let's call," Ian urged.

Mom slouched in her chair. "Go ahead, but I know she'll just scold me."

Dad took Mom's hand, his thumb stroking her fingers. "Will you bring us the phone, Robin?"

I got the telephone from the hall and brought it into the kitchen. Mom and Dad were simply holding hands and smiling at each other. It was such a pretty picture that I wanted to make it last for as long as I could, so I dialed for them.

"Hello?" Grandmother answered.

"This is Robin. Please don't hang up," I said desperately.

"Why would I do that?" She sounded surprisingly cheerful for someone who had just lost her boyfriend.

I didn't want to explain why in front of my parents, so I asked her how she was feeling.

"Tip-top," she said. "I've been out to a garage sale with Madame. She's here now, having a cup of tea."

I felt an immense sense of relief that Grandmother wasn't retreating into a shell after Wolf had run away. And I know my ballet teacher had missed her expeditions with my grandmother. "Any good bargains?" I teased.

"I got a coat that was such a steal, Madame says I should be arrested," Grandmother boasted.

I chatted with her a little longer and then glanced at my parents. Mom looked a little scared. "You ask," she said softly, chickening out.

Taking a breath, I got to the point. "We were wondering if Mom could stay home today."

There was a long silence at the other end of the line. At first, I cringed, thinking that Mom was right and that I was going to get a long lecture on family obligations. Instead, Grandmother said, "Sometimes you can take a lovely flower from a Chinese garden and plant it here, and you get a strange weed. Just because it does well at home doesn't mean that it does well here."

"Well, maybe it needs the right plant food. We can go over to the Botanical Gardens sometime and get advice."

Grandmother chuckled. "That's not what I meant. Let me speak to your mother."

"Grandmother wants to talk to you," I said, passing the receiver over to Mom.

"Hello," Mom said nervously as she took it. After a moment, she said, "But they can't afford to replace me. Well, yes . . . no . . . yes . . ." Finally she held the receiver away from her and examined it before she spoke into it again. "Are you sure you're my mother? All right. I'll leave it to you."

When she hung up, she seemed dazed. "Well," Dad demanded, "what did your mother say?"

"She said I could take as many days off as I like," Mom said in amazement.

Dad sat back, just as surprised. "Robin, are you sure you dialed the right number?"

I knew Grandmother was feeling great, but I hadn't

thought she felt *that* great. "Maybe it's a grandmother from a parallel universe, like in the comic books."

Mom still stared at the telephone as if she thought it had malfunctioned.

"That's wonderful news, honey," Dad said and kissed her. He hadn't called her that in a long time—let alone kiss her.

As Dad called up Gasser's, I started to wash the dishes. All that time, I tried to figure out what was going on, but I wasn't any closer to an answer when the telephone rang again. "Hello?" I said, picking up the receiver, but there was silence at the other end.

Mom and Dad had shifted into the living room to finish reading the newspaper. And I got ready to tell Dad we had some kind of weirdo on the phone.

Suddenly a pleasant, thin voice began to sing, "I love a lady far away . . ."

It was Wolf. I clutched the receiver. "You're not in jail, are you?"

"No," he chuckled. "We met Ah Wing in the street. He was driving around looking for parking so he helped us get away."

Good old reliable Ah Wing. That was a relief. "How did you get my number?"

"I called up the family association," Wolf said. "They still had your number from the time you called them."

"Let me give you Grandmother's number." My mind had gone blank suddenly.

"No," Wolf said anxiously, "we don't have a lot of time. Our train leaves soon."

"Our train?" I asked excitedly. "Did you find your daughter?" I added. "I mean, your real one."

His voice was as warm and affectionate as ever. "As far as I'm concerned, I have two daughters. You are the younger one. But I'm leaving with your older sister. There is a lot to make up for."

I thought of that angry woman and shivered. It wasn't a fate I would choose. If I had turned out like her, I wouldn't have blamed my real dad if he had run in the opposite direction.

"Where are you going?" I asked.

"I can't say," he said sadly. "This has to be my one and only call. I don't want to get you involved with the immigration authorities. They'll soon be snooping all around."

The news sank in slowly. In a modern world that boasted so many different means of communication, there seemed something terribly wrong about a wall of silence. We might have been living a hundred years ago, with me standing in the village and waving good-bye as he sailed off to America.

"Please call Grandmother," I begged.

"Tell her I love her, too," he said. In the background some depot loudspeaker began to announce destinations. When he began to sing again, he did it in a louder voice, but it made him a little off-key.

"I love a lady far away.
   She never eats. She pines all day.
   When she's asleep, she dreams of me—
   The man who lives across the sea.

"Let's trade places, Madame Moon,
   So I can see her very soon.
   I'll touch her tears with my bright light.
   And make them pearls for her delight."

I was so choked up that it took me a moment to say,
"Don't go."
   But he had already hung up.

NINETEEN

Beauty

When I finished the dishes, I went into my bedroom and sat, staring out the window. I remembered what Wolf had once said about beauty. I don't think I had understood it until now. The friendship between Grandmother and Wolf had been something lovely— like a crown made out of crystal and gold wire that shone with light and happiness. But it was never really made for stiff, clumsy human fingers. The moment I tried to grab the crown for Wolf and Grandmother, I broke it. And that brought back the aching inside.

Or like Wolf's real daughter, my "older sister." First she had dreamed of finding her father and then of reaching America, and she hadn't been happy when either dream came true.

Suddenly, I found myself lifting my arms and rising from my bed. I started my moon dance, feeling clumsy at first because I hadn't warmed up.

I found my body had a will of its own. I went beyond the steps I had done that other moonlit night. I raised my hands as if shaping a giant moon overhead. One that I wanted to embrace.

And I began to dance for my Grandmother. For Wolf. For all those who had waited so long to reach for their dreams.

"Wonderful, Robin," Madame said. Her r's rolled thickly from her tongue.

I turned, breathless and a little ashamed. My door was half open, and Grandmother was standing with her canes in one hand and the other on the doorknob. Behind her was Madame herself with a bag in either hand. Beyond them were Dad, Mom, and Ian.

"Th-thank you, Madame," I stammered.

"Yes, it was beautiful," Grandmother said proudly.

"May we come in?" Madame asked.

"Yes, please do." I began grabbing stray clothes off the floor.

Grandmother came in on her canes, followed by the rest. "Sit," she said to Mom and Dad, pointing at the bed with a cane. Ian flopped down on the floor at their feet.

Grandmother cleared her throat. "I've spoken to Eddy and Georgie. It's time they hired a bookkeeper," she said to Mom. "Consider this your official notice that you are no longer employed at the store."

"I've been fired." Mom grew giddy as the news sank

in. "I've been fired." She began to laugh with relief. "I've been fired."

"Things have changed back in China. Times change. And people change with the times," Grandmother said, quoting the waiter. "Family should always be important, but nowadays you don't have to sacrifice everything for them."

It took a moment for Grandmother's new views to sink in. "But how are Eddy and Georgie going to manage without me?" Mom asked.

Grandmother laughed. "I live under Eddy, so I can hear him every time he goes out to eat. He and Marilyn dine at too many expensive restaurants for people with a new store. They can stay home and cook instead. With the money they save, they can hire a full-time bookkeeper."

"You're going to make their meals." Mom brightened.

"No," Grandmother said with a firm shake of her head. "I have my own life. I'm going to stop going to the store, too."

Mom's jaw dropped. "What made you decide that?"

"I saw how a friend's family treated him," Grandmother said with a wink at me. "And I decided that I wouldn't let that happen to me."

Mom threw her arms around Grandmother. "Thank you."

When Mom let go, Grandmother patted her on the hip. "Now you go somewhere with your husband for a few hours. I'll watch the children. But just be sure to be back by six."

"Are you sure?" Mom asked.

"See a movie, have a fancy coffee. Just go," Grandmother ordered. "Or don't you remember what to do?"

Dad scratched the back of his head sheepishly. "As it happens, I can't recall the last time we had an afternoon by ourselves."

Grandmother gave him a poke with her cane. "You'll think of something once you're outside."

Dad held up his hands with a bubbly laugh. "We're gone."

When we heard the door slam behind them, I helped Grandmother sit down on my bed. "I wish you'd come up here ten minutes earlier. I just heard from Wolf," I said and paused, glancing at Madame.

"Don't worry. Your grandmother has told me all about him," Madame assured me.

"Well, she didn't tell me," Ian said annoyed.

"Later," I said to him, "in about ten years."

"Ah Wing managed to spirit Wolf and his daughter away," I explained to Grandmother.

I expected her to be upset, but she merely heaved a large sigh. "I hope they finally find happiness together."

I was afraid that she was trying to hide her feelings as she had hidden them from her mother when she was a little girl. "It's okay to cry," I said gently.

She refused the box of tissues that I held out to her. "A door opens and a door closes. I took that to heart."

Bored with all the talk about unfamiliar people, Ian peered hopefully into one of the shopping bags. "Any toys?"

"Show them the coat," Madame urged.

As I set the tissue box on my bed, Grandmother eased a satin brocade coat from an old Emporium bag. It was teal with butterflies all over it. Lifting it up, she held it against herself. "Well, what do you think?" she asked shyly.

"It looks pretty," I said and added hastily, "and stylish." As I pressed its shoulders and sleeves against her, Ian left in disgust. In a moment, I could hear the Wolf Warriors on television. He must have put in one of his tapes.

Grandmother studied herself in the mirror. "You think so?"

"It will be perfect for the occasion," Madame said with a nod of her head.

"Did you get it to wear for something?" I asked.

"No," Grandmother said coyly.

I had another happy thought. "You're taking Grandmother to the ballet," I said to Madame.

"Sometime I will," Madame said, "but we have no specific plans." She was enjoying having a secret just as much as Grandmother was.

I guessed I must be getting dense in my old age. "Well, what did you get the coat for, then?"

"Mr. White Whiskers—I mean Ah Wing—asked me to go out." She looked embarrassed as she restored the coat to the bag. "I don't know where we're going, but he promised it would be someplace nice."

"You've got a date," I said, stunned.

"It's not a date," she protested, but though she was trying her best to appear calm, she could barely conceal her excitement. Madame and Grandmother together reminded me of myself with Amy and Leah. "Yes, it is," Madame insisted.

"Well, don't tell anyone," Grandmother warned me, "especially your mother. She never could keep a secret. One time when I made a mistake and washed a pair of red socks with the underwear, she told all her neighbors that her brothers wore pink underwear."

Well, Ah Wing wasn't as imaginative as Wolf, but he was cheerful and kind. Wolf was the kind of person who might design clocks, but Ah Wing was the type who built them and kept them running.

I couldn't resist asking, "Who are you going to be this time?"

Grandmother gave me a pinch. "Myself, of course."

"Well, then, you'll need earrings to match your coat." I went to my bureau and opened the top drawer. From it I took the red silk pouch with the jade earrings Wolf had tried to give her. Opening the pouch, I shook them onto my palm. "I got these on loan from a special friend, but I guess she'd trust you."

It took Grandmother's eyes a moment to focus on the earrings. "Oh, yes," she said.

I held them up against her ears. "I think they're a perfect match."

She bit her lip nervously. "You don't think I'll look silly wearing them?" I suppose she still associated them with her girlhood.

"Your butterfly days are just starting."

"Ha, ha. How droll," Grandmother said, but she took the small gold posts from her ears. Her fingers, though, had trouble with the pins.

"Let me do that," Madame said, eagerly taking the earrings from her and opening them.

When Grandmother had put the earrings on, she studied their effect on the image in the mirror. "They make my face look pale, don't you think?"

"Mom has some blush," I said, and went and got it.

When I came back, Madame and Grandmother were studying the mirror as excitedly as two girls.

What if Sleeping Beauty had not been able to stay the same? What if she had aged instead? There would have been a teenage heart in an older body when she woke up. Maybe I had my own Sleeping Beauty on my hands—one that I had helped rouse.

As I put the blush on the table, I rested my cheek against Grandmother's. For a moment, our reflections hovered in the mirror, her face and mine. The color of the skin and hair might have been different, but the faces were the same. Same chin. Same cheeks. Same broad forehead. When Grandmother was twelve, she probably looked like me. And when I got to be her age, I would look like her.

It was time to wake my Sleeping Beauty. It was time to celebrate.

"How about trying your hair like this?" I suggested. Grandmother waited expectantly while I reached for my brush.

It was butterfly time.

AFTERWORD

While we were developing my stage adaptation of *Dragonwings* at the Sundance Institute, the play's director, Phyllis S. K. Look, and I researched some of the historical background. We learned that there was a time when there were many Chinese men who—like Wolf—had left their wives to work in America.

One of the actors, Marcelo Tubert, then told us that we had helped to illuminate an odd experience from his boyhood. When he was a child growing up in Los Angeles, one of his best friends had been a Chinese-American boy. One day, Marcelo and this friend had been recruited to pretend to be the sons of a restaurant cook—even though Marcelo did not look Asian at all. The boys never went back to the restaurant but Marcelo had never forgotten that sad, desperate old man, and after hearing Marcelo's story neither could I.

Then, a little while later, I saw a story on a national

newscast about a new service in Japan. It seems that men and women in Japan are so busy working that they do not have time to visit their elderly parents. A company sprung up to rectify the situation. For a fee, the company sends actors to visit the parents and pose as their grown-up children. One such visit had been videotaped. The elderly parents were quite sane and knew at one level that the actors were actors, yet in their loneliness they found it nice to pretend that the visitors were their real children. And at the end, the parents sent the actors away loaded down with gifts of food.

The news story shone a gentler light upon the madness of a lonely old cook who was ending his last years in some tiny, greasy kitchen in Chinatown.